THE GENETIC BUCCANEER

A "Cap Kennedy" Novel

by

GREGORY KERN

DAW BOOKS, INC.
DONALD A. WOLLHEIM, PUBLISHER

1301 Avenue of the Americas
New York, N. Y. 10019

Published by
THE NEW AMERICAN LIBRARY
OF CANADA LIMITED

Cover art by Jack Gaughan.

FIRST PRINTING, OCTOBER 1974

1 2 3 4 5 6 7 8 9

PRINTED IN CANADA
COVER PRINTED IN U.S.A.

THE OFFER THAT COULD NOT BE REFUSED

"A man can respect a worthy adversary, Captain, and you have shown yourself to be that," said Kaifeng to Cap Kennedy. "But what has it gained you? What can Terran Control with all its wealth and power give you? You will always have superiors. You will never be allowed to form your own destiny. At each turn your fate will be decided by others.

"Fate, Captain, an irony when you think about it. On Sheol you gambled and yet what did you win? The life of a friend—and where is that friend now? I also gambled and received the potential mastery of the universe. I am willing to gamble again. Join me. Work with me. Share in what is to come."

"Just what are you offering?" Kennedy said slowly.

"An empire!" Kaifeng drew in his breath, seeming to expand, to grow even taller, a man entranced. "Worlds for your playthings, women, luxuries, men to command. More wealth and power than you have ever imagined—all will be yours if you obey me. You have an imagination, Captain, use it! Earth itself could be your footstool."

CHAPTER ONE

The spaceport at Krome was busy and the receptionist at the transient hotel had little time to spare for the nondescript man who claimed his attention.

"Corade? Sure, room seven-thirty-two. I'll announce you. Name?"

"Dene Winguard. I'm from the *Shardorn,* his vessel."

"Crewmate, uh?" The receptionist turned from the phone. "Go on up, he's expecting you."

Corade was a big man with a shock of reddish hair, blue eyes, the shoulders of a bull and a thin scar tracing its way over one cheek. He wore the puce and green of the Rumzan Line, his insignia the electronic flash of a communications officer. He yelled to enter at the knock on his door, then turned from his packing. He narrowed his eyes at the visitor.

"You're not Dene. Say, what is this?"

The stranger carefully closed and locked the door. Corade straightened, his hands clenching a little, body tensed for action. As he stepped forward the man quickly said, "There's no need for alarm. I had to use a subterfuge in order to see you. I've come with a business proposition."

Corade relaxed, thinking he knew the answer. He had been approached before on a dozen different worlds.

"Smuggling? If so forget it. We're headed for Weingold. They check and double check and the penalties are too high."

"Not smuggling." The man stepped close, lifting his hand. "This."

He wore an ornate ring bright with a glittering gem. As Corade looked at the jewel it seemed to expand, to open like a flower, releasing a gush of acrid vapor. Even as he smelled it he fell, dead before he reached the floor.

Ten minutes later the receptionist looked up and smiled.

"Checking out, Mr. Corade?"

"Not exactly." The big red-headed man returned the smile, hefting the bag he was carrying. "There's been a delay, that's why Dene came to see me. I'll just drop this off at the ship and carry on with some unfinished business." His wink left no doubt as to its nature. "We pull out early tomorrow, so I'll keep the room another day. Make out the bill and I'll settle it now to save trouble."

It was considerate, but then Corade always was: the kind of resident the hotel liked, quiet, discreet as to his pleasures, no trouble at all.

As he counted the money the receptionist said, "A moment, sir, you've got change coming."

"Keep it." Corade added another bill to the rest. "Give this to the chambermaid. No need for her to go into the room—it might be a little embarrassing." Another wink.

"I understand." The receptionist deftly pocketed his tip. "If I don't see you again, sir, have a good trip. Will we have the pleasure of your company when you are on Krome next?"

"Sure. You can rely on it."

The big man moved quickly from the hotel toward the spaceport, hearing an irate voice as he reached one of the ships on the field.

"For Pete's sake, Corade! The old man's hopping. What kept you?"

"Does it matter? I'm here."

"And none too soon." The second officer jerked his thumb at the open lock behind him. "Get on duty fast! We're due to lift within the hour."

The *Shardorn* was a vessel of the Delta class, plying

a regular route among a handful of worlds, carrying light freight and passengers. The big man dumped his bag in a cabin he shared with the second engineer and went to the communications shack. It was empty—the *Shardorn* carried only one electronics officer—and he sat before the panel making the routine checks.

An hour later, all ports sealed, crew at their stations, the vessel lifted. Three hours after that the redhead made an adjustment to the hybeam receiver. Two hours later he had an interview with Captain Schleheim.

"You were late reporting for duty, Corade. Why?"

"I'm sorry, sir. I was delayed."

"That is no excuse. It is my standing order that every man be at his post at least two hours before lift. This is the second time you've flouted that order. Do it again and you'll be looking for another ship."

"It won't happen again, sir."

"You know what to expect if it does. As it is you lose a day's pay."

Corade would have been resentful; the big man's hands closed into fists where they hung at his sides. Schleheim noticed the gesture and his craggy face hardened. An old veteran of space, tough as the metal which enclosed his tiny world, he ran a hard ship.

"Two days' pay," he corrected. "And, by God, if you lift a hand to me you'll spend the journey in irons."

The hands opened, the blue eyes looked down at the deck between them.

"I'm sorry, sir. But two days' pay for an hour's lateness? It seems unfair."

"Whine and it'll be worse. Now get the hell out of my sight."

After he left, the first officer turned from where he'd been monitoring the instruments, the screens which showed the star-shot vista of space.

"That's odd, Captain. The last time you chewed Corade out he tried to make a joke of it. I never expected him to complain. Maybe he's losing his sense of humor?"

"He'll lose more than that if he doesn't get a grip on himself," snapped Schleheim. "An officer's entitled to his fun, but not when it interferes with the operation of my ship." He dismissed the incident with a shrug. With the vessel traveling at plus-C velocity he had other things to worry about than a girl-bemused spaceman . . . the passengers, for one.

Tradition demanded that he make the routine circuit, dropping a word, exchanging greetings, letting them know their lives were in good hands. More than that, though, he liked to know the people he was carrying: the entrepreneur already busy with a host of plans, the three dancers, gay, lithe young things whose conversation rose like the twitter of birds, the solemn woman with the peaked face and gemmed insignia—an officer of the Matriarch of Weingold, the scatter of others.

He paused by a high-backed chair, leaning with slight deference toward the woman it contained. Laura Previn was still attractive despite her years, the figure beneath the plain gown curved and lush. With cosmetics and a more decorative gown she would have rivaled any of the dancers, but then, he reminded himself, he was regarding her from the viewpoint of maturity, not of youth.

"A pleasure to have you with us, madam," he said sincerely. "It isn't often that my ship carries a genetic engineer as noted as yourself."

She returned his smile. "You flatter me, Captain."

"I speak the truth. Your work on selected physical types will open new worlds for habitation and what you have already accomplished in the field of revivication is of personal interest to all spacemen. Even I, a crusty old man, can recognize that."

She smiled, making no comment, and he sensed her desire to be alone. Sighing, he made the rounds of the other passengers, wondering what it would be like to be married to such a woman, to share, even remotely, in her work. On his return she halted him with a touch on his arm.

"Captain, how long will this journey take?"

"Ten days, madam." She should have known, but genius was noted for absentmindedness. "I shall make them as comfortable for you as I can," he promised. "Anything you need, anything you want, simply ask."

"That is kind of you."

"If you care to inspect the ship I shall be happy to escort you."

This was a measure of his regard. Passengers would normally be a nuisance to such a man, certainly not to be shown around. Yet the workings of a vessel did not interest her; she tried to soften her rejection.

"Perhaps later, Captain, but I do have work to get on with. Notes for my speech at the conference and other things."

"Dinner then?" His relief was skillfully masked. "It would honor me to have you share my table."

This arrangement lasted five days, artificial divisions of time which darkened the ship at regular intervals, brightened it at others—a device to avoid the hazard of time-disorientation. On returning to the bridge after a meal Schleheim found the second engineer waiting for him.

"What is it, Grixon?"

The man cleared his throat. "Something odd, sir. About Corade. I don't really know how to say it."

"Get on with it, man!"

"Well, we've shared a cabin for some time now and you get to know a man's ways. Corade likes to joke and tell yarns about women. At least he did. This trip he's barely spoken to me. And another thing. He used to snore like the devil. Now he doesn't. And I owed him some money; when I mentioned it to him he didn't seem to know what I was talking about. Little things, sir, but they add up."

"To what?"

"I don't know," Grixon confessed. "It's just a feeling I have. That I'm sharing my cabin with a stranger. I thought I'd better report it."

"You did right."

Schleheim was a conscientious man; he dutifully recorded the interview in the log, making a mental note to keep an eye on Corade. The man was a good enough communications officer, but he was nothing special and could always be replaced. If he stepped out of line just one more time that's exactly what would happen.

Alone in his cabin the big red-headed man looked at his watch. It was no ordinary timepiece, but spelled out the days, hours, minutes and split seconds on a graduated scale. This chronometer had cost more than any officer could earn in half a year; it was powered by dying atoms and was accurate to a fraction of a second over a century.

Grixon was on duty; from behind the bulkhead against the big man's head came a soft inhalation from sleeping men, stewards now relieved of watch. It was far into the night, the passengers were in their cabins, the salon deserted. Two minutes and it would be time to act.

He took several items from his bag, a compact piece of equipment, a needle gun firing lethal darts, a heavy Dione, the barrel finned, the orifice flared. Cracking the door, he entered the passage and turned toward the engine room. The door was fast. He opened it, smiled at the crewman who turned toward him, and fired the needler at his throat.

The man hit a tool rack as he fell, metal clashing as it followed him to the floor.

"Cran?" Footsteps echoed from behind the humped bulk of the engines. "You clumsy idiot! Can't you watch what you're doing?" Grixon came into view, eyes widening as he saw the fallen man, the tools scattered around him.

"Cran! What's wrong?" His voice changed as he ran forward. "Corade! What the hell are you doing here?"

Again the needler spat its silent death.

The big man was hard at work before Grixon had fallen. He used tools from the scattered heap to tear at the engine casing, opening it to reveal bunched wires. He picked at these, hooking the compact mechanism he carried into the circuit, setting it with deft touches. He then moved to another part of the engine, tearing away the seals of the manual override. He glanced at his watch as he waited, tense, the needler held ready. Three minutes later he adjusted the bared controls, killing all maneuverability and drive.

In the control room Schleheim noticed nothing, the instruments still registering as they should, his attention claimed by the first officer standing at the Larvic-Shaw spatial disturbance detector.

"Captain. Something close."

The screen, normally a fuzz of gently drifting lines from the activity of distant suns, was now writhing with a complex mesh of curves centering in a convoluted node —a sure sign that the nearby normal continuum had been disrupted by irregular energies. It could mean an electronic storm, rogue matter still beyond normal detector range, a rift in the space-time fabric causing opposed forces to swirl in a conglomeration of three-dimensional fields—or, incredibly, another vessel dangerously close.

But nothing showed in the screens.

Schleheim stared at them, uneasily conscious that something was wrong. Plumping into the control chair, he made adjustments. The *Shardorn* should have turned, lifted, raced away from the potential danger revealed on the Larvic-Shaw. Instead nothing happened. The instruments remained as they were, false readings which proved the vessel was dead beneath his hands.

"Captain!" Roston's voice was an echo of his own disbelief. "For God's sake, what is it?"

Something huge suddenly shimmered in the screens as if covered with a fine blue mist, the blueness quickly vanishing to reveal a glimmering shape which reflected the cold light of the stars, the bulk of the *Shardorn* itself. As they watched it came closer, matching velocity and direction. A dull thud vibrated through the hull as the two ships touched.

"An attack!" Observed fact blasted aside the captain's incredulity. "Sound the alarm!"

Laura Previn heard it as the door of her cabin crashed open to reveal a big man with a shock of red hair, his lips smiling, the Dione in his hand giving the lie to his apparent good humor.

"Up!" he snapped. "Quickly."

"What—"

"Don't argue, woman! Do as I say." He ripped a thin, transparent space suit from the emergency locker, dropping its twin from under his free arm. "Put it on and seal it tight. Damn you, do it!"

She stood for a moment and then the Dione lifted, the finned barrel with its flared orifice leveling on her legs. A touch on the trigger and released energy would spout from the disintegration of the unstable charge, forces focused and controlled by the ring of permanent magnets in the barrel. The naked energy produced could incinerate a horse, would sear the flesh from her legs and leave nothing but charred bone.

"Put on that suit," said the big man. "Do it now or I'll fire and then do it for you. This is your last chance."

Shaking, she obeyed. He donned his own suit while she was busy, then snapped tight both final seals.

"And now what?" Her voice was flat as it vibrated the diaphragm set into the mask. "Has the ship been holed?"

For answer he turned and fired at the junction of the closed door. Metal turned molten beneath the blast, then fused and cooled again in a tough weld.

"Just a precaution," he said casually. "We don't want any fool bursting in here and trying to act the hero, do we?"

"What is this all about?"

"You'll see in good time."

She was tall and strong, and an academic life hadn't spoiled her vitality. He grunted as she lunged toward him, one hand knocking aside the Dione, the other tearing at his mask. His features seemed to blur beneath her hand, to soften and take a different shape, then he had pushed her back and was as before.

But the glimpse had been enough.

"You're not human," she said. "You're a Mimic. A Mimic from Dephene."

He bowed mockingly.

"What do you want with me?"

"All in good time, madam. Now we wait."

They waited as the lock was forced and men poured

into the *Shardorn,* weapons blazing, burning the air, the passengers, the hapless crew. Cursing, Schleheim tore at the locked arms cabinet, throwing a Dione to Roston, taking another himself. Carried only for use in the remote possibility of mutiny, the weapons were mostly meant to awe rather than injure. He ignored the needlers loaded with their anesthetic darts: his ship had been boarded, he was in no mood to be gentle.

A man died as he fired, a second, and then Schleheim himself was wreathed in flame, shafts of energy spearing his torso, his stomach, charring lungs and intestines, bursting through pelvis and spine. He went down in a smoking heap of unrecognizable tissue.

Roston joined him, together with the passengers and the rest of the crew. Only one man did not die immediately.

First Engineer Holtac had been partially protected by a half-open door when the raiders raced toward the engine room. He had lost his left arm and half the shoulder. When a second blast cut the legs from under him he fell into a pool of his own blood, incredibly surviving the initial shock. The searing blasts, deflected, had served to cauterize the wounds. Lying, tormented with pain, the scent of his own burned flesh heavy in his nostrils, he could do nothing but wait as seeping blood drained away his life.

The noise faded, the screams, the roar of Diones. The following orders were snapped in cold, emotionless tones.

Holtac felt a grate of transmitted vibration and the thin, horrifying hiss of escaping air. Like a crippled snail he crawled into the engine room, reaching the mechanism the big man had planted there, tearing free the wires and inching on to another device the raiders had left attached to the main pile. A jerk and it too was free, and he fell, rolling, red stabs of pain tearing at his consciousness.

Yet there was still something he had to do.

The destructive device had been disconnected. The automatic alarm beacon incorporated into the vessel would already be sending out its signal of distress. If he could manage to get into a suit, seal it tight, obtain a large supply of extra air, find drugs to kill his pain, to halt the internal bleeding, find water and antibiotics, he might, just might, stand a slender chance of rescue.

But with only one arm and no legs, with blackness edging his vision and weakness sapping what was left of his strength, it was an impossible task.

And he was a gambler who knew the odds.

Painfully, dipping his finger in his own blood to use as ink, he began to draw a pattern on the deck next to his face. He was still drawing when he died.

CHAPTER TWO

The park was a green jewel set in the heart of the city, one of a number placed among the soaring buildings of Newark, the capital of Earth. The small area was landscaped with flowering trees and gardens bright with diverse hues, a pool in which fish sported and fountains played, benches on which the old could sit and dream, the young pause and enjoy pastoral charm. There were terraces too, on which lovers could stroll, and meandering ways and shadowed paths leading to sculptured glades.

Kennedy found it charming.

He strolled slowly along one of the terraces, apparently casually, yet his eyes were restless as he looked from side to side, weighing, evaluating with practiced ease. He scanned the men who walked past or who lingered without apparent reason; the women who stared, young girls who slowed as he neared, bold eyes searching his face, his body.

One said something to her friend, then sighed enviously and walked on with dragging reluctance. She would like to have stayed, to have talked to the tall man with the broad shoulders and narrow waist, to have turned a casual meeting into something with deeper meaning.

An outworlder, she thought, but no, his face bore the unmistakable stamp of earth. Possibly a spaceman, she considered, but certainly not less than an officer. And yet he wore no uniform. His blouse and pants were of nacreous whiteness, shimmering with glowing color, the tracery of thin black lines accentuating the richness of the material.

A wealthy man, she decided, a dilettante of sorts, one devoted to sport and physical pursuits, a hunter or an adventurer who had trodden strange worlds and seen exotic places.

One day, perhaps, she would do the same.

Kennedy reached the end of the terrace, turned, walked back to pause and lean on the parapet of the wall along the side. He looked down at the sward below, at the pool of tinkling water and the fountain of rainbow spray.

Close to the fountain sat a mother with her child, a sturdy boy of six or seven, neat in a miniature play-uniform of blue, green and silver, already dreaming of commanding a Mobile Aid Laboratory and Construction Authority, one of the MALACAs which guarded Earth and the planets in the Terran Sphere of Influence, the complex ruled and guided by Terran Control.

The boy's shrill voice rose above the tinkle of water.

"But Mother, I don't understand. If Earth owns all the planets then why do we have enemies?"

"Earth doesn't own them all," she said patiently. "In fact we don't own any but the worlds of our own system, certain uninhabited planets and those we have directly colonized. The other worlds in the Terran Sphere are our allies. We help them and protect them when they need either."

"Against the Chambodians?"

"Them and others. Space is full of worlds and races. There are groups and empires and conclaves of all sizes. How did your tutor tell you to think of inhabited space?"

"Like a bunch of fruit," the boy said instantly. "A big bowl of grapes."

"Not grapes," she corrected. "That would mean every unit is the same size, and they aren't. A bowl of fruit, rather, apples and pears, bananas and pineapples, nuts and grapes and oranges, all lying close to each other but never merging. And don't forget the spaces in between, the areas of scattered planets, independent and alone, or places where there are no habitable worlds at all."

A good analogy, thought the listening Kennedy, and she bettered it, using easily observable facts to bolster the abstraction.

"Like that." She pointed to where a vendor of balloons stood with his pole, the slender shaft thick with brightly colored shapes of all sizes. "But don't worry about it now. You'll learn all about it later on."

"When I enter the Academy?"

"Yes, darling." For a moment her face shadowed with the realization that soon her boy would grow into a man, would leave her to make his own way. And then she smiled, knowing it had to be. "Now go and play while I read Daddy's letter."

A spacewife with her man posted somewhere close, perhaps on the Moon, Kennedy supposed, working a three-month shift with extended leaves. Terran Control was reluctant to separate families with young children for extensive periods.

"Cap! Sorry I'm late."

Kennedy had seen Weyburn come down the terrace, only moving his eyes as the man settled his weight on the coping at his side. Still not turning, Kennedy said, "There are three men watching us. They've been tailing me since I arrived."

"Describe them." Weyburn pursed his lips as Kennedy gave the details. "Sloppy workmanship. I'll have to crack down on them."

"Your men?"

"There are two others, one a woman." Weyburn straightened and glanced casually around. "The man reading a book by the balloon seller and that girl who seems to be waiting for a friend. You didn't spot them because they've only just arrived. I had them checking around to spot if anyone had followed me."

"Trouble?"

"Spring cleaning." Weyburn was curt. "I'm having the office checked for bugs and plants. Unnecessary, maybe, but I want to be sure."

Weyburn always wanted to be sure. The Director of Terran Control lived up to his appearance, the prominent nose and lined cheeks together with the hooded eyes giving him the likeness of a brooding eagle. A man who never took anything for granted, he had learned long ago the truth engraved on the plaque resting on his desk—the seven words which no Terran could ever afford to forget:

Eternal vigilance is the price of liberty.

He said, "Let's find somewhere we can talk."

They picked a bench beneath a flowering tree, placed in a curve of a narrow path so it could not be seen by anyone not also in view. As they sat a man drifted past, his face in a book; another took an unusual interest in the antics of a nesting bird. Both remained well beyond earshot. The others would too, the silent, unobtrusive guards making sure that Kennedy and Weyburn would not be disturbed, just like a pair of ordinary civilians engaged in casual conversation.

"Trouble, Cap." The Director came immediately to the point. "The *Shardorn* was boarded, gutted, wrecked and damn near destroyed on a journey from Krome to Weingold. If it hadn't been for luck and the guts of one man we'd never have known anything about it. A bomb had been rigged to trigger a burn-out from the pile and another electronic device would have created a feedback to vaporize the entire ship. Holtac managed to abort the intention."

"Holtac?"

"The first engineer. He's dead. When he freed the gimmick from the electronic circuits the automatic beacon resumed operation. MALACA 8 was close, so Commander Mbomoma dispatched a unit to investigate. The *Shardorn* was in the Yenisey Region, but what the hell? A distress call has to be answered. There were a few ruffled feathers but Weit managed to smooth them down."

Conrad Weit, head of Diplomacy, was good at that.

"The *Shardorn?*" Kennedy asked. "Isn't that a ship of the Rumzan Line?"

"A Delta class operating in the Yenisey Region. Captain Schleheim was in command. Did you know him?"

Kennedy nodded, remembering the tough veteran, his reputation for running a tight ship. How had such a man lost his command? And why had it been done at all?

"You said the ship had been boarded. Are you sure of that?"

"I'm sure." Weyburn was grim. "I know it sounds incredible, but it happened. And because of Holtac's courage we can figure out how it was done. Someone fed a false-information device into the circuitry, then killed velocity and maneuverability. Schleheim wouldn't have known what was happening until it was too late. He might have had a brief warning from the Larvic-Shaw, but that was all. And even if he received warning there was nothing he could do about it. The ship was dead."

"Which meant there had to be a saboteur aboard," said Kennedy. "Schleheim would never have allowed any passenger free run of the ship, so it would have to be a member of the crew. But his men were carefully selected; he would never tolerate anyone suspicious. A stranger would have been watched and his things searched—Schleheim was known for his detestation of smuggling. So how did that electronic device get aboard?" He answered his own question. "A switch, it had to be."

A pebble lay on the ground; Weyburn kicked at it, his face savage.

"You're right, Cap. Seven hours after the *Shardorn* left Krome a dead man was discovered in Corade's room at the transient hotel. He was the communications officer. At first the police thought it was him—the face and hands had been dissolved by acid—but then the receptionist remembered talking to him when he left. He could have returned, of course, but we know better. Someone impersonated him. That person wrecked the hybeam receiver on the ship so no warning message could be registered. He wouldn't have worried about the one sent ahead to Weingold—he didn't intend getting there."

"A Mimic," said Kennedy. "That or an accomplished actor with a good knowledge of ship routine and electronics. Such a man wouldn't come cheap. What were they after? The cargo?"

"No." Again Weyburn kicked at the pebble. "The *Shardorn* was carrying Laura Previn from Krome to Weingold. She had been invited to attend a conference on life-manipulation and allied subjects. She is probably the most skilled genetics engineer there is." He handed Kennedy a photograph. "This is what they did to get her."

Kennedy looked at it and saw a scene of desolation: Bodies lying, torn, burned, unrecognizable heaps of seared and charred tissue. His hands tightened a little, anger at the wanton butchery hardening the lines and planes of his face, turning his mouth into something cruel.

"Thirty-six passengers and crew," said Weyburn bitterly. "Three young dancers, a child of eight going to meet her mother, two brothers on their way to retirement, a pregnant woman . . ." He broke off, breathing hard. "All dead, Cap. All burned down with Diones."

"All?"

"The bodies tally. Thirty-six people left Krome, thirty-six bodies were found. But there was one man more than there should have been, one woman less. Laura Previn."

"You're certain?"

"Commander Mbomoma wasn't close by accident, Cap. He'd been ordered to keep watch and knew what to look for. The suit was gone from her cabin and she'd been clever. There were some markings on the bulkhead, a name, the word 'forced.' I guess whoever was responsible felt it safe to be careless. After all, as far as he knew, the entire ship was destined to turn into a luminous cloud. And there was something else. Two of the bodies, both male, had been wearing material different from uniform fabric. And two men in the bridge, the captain and his first officer, were armed."

Schleheim would have put up a fight if given the chance, Kennedy knew. He leaned back, eyes narrowed with thought, visualizing exactly what must have happened, yet puzzled by apparent contradictions. Why the butchery if the ship was to be exploded later? A subtle gas would have served the same purpose as the Diones if the intention had merely been to kill. And why had the dead boarders been left to bring the dead-count up to the necessary total?

A precaution in case anything went wrong? A smoke-screen to hide the real intent?

And why Weyburn's interest?

Piracy was everyone's business—such scum had to be eliminated whenever and wherever they appeared—but that was the job of the regular forces. Terran Control could only offer to help, never demand or insist in the spaces outside the Terran Sphere. And such aid would be offered by Jud Harbin, the Military Commander of Terran Forces, not by the Director, who mostly worked in the dark.

Kennedy knew there were things he hadn't been told yet: the details which made the incident the province of the Free Acting Terran Envoys, of which he was the foremost. The business of FATE was to maintain the galactic peace at all times regardless of cost, to manipulate, investigate and prevent the smoldering flames of potential war from breaking out into a holocaust of mass destruction . . . to kill if that was the only means of avoiding the danger.

High voices echoed down the path and a girl came into view bouncing a brightly colored ball. She was small, a ribbon in her hair, cheeks ruddy with the glow of health. Behind her came the mother, an elder edition of the mite, pushing a baby in a carriage. Kennedy caught the ball as it bounced toward him, smiled and tossed it gently into the outstretched pudgy hands.

"Thank you, mister."

Kennedy watched as the little party moved on, the girl busy with her ball. The happy, contented scene reminded him of how people were now at peace after millennia of pain and blood and sweat—the price paid by their forebears. Calm prosperity finally ruled Earth.

And Kennedy was dedicated to maintaining that peace.

It was all around him, in the park, the city, the nations united under ORDER, the government of Earth.

The Overall Regulation Department of Environmental Recourses had turned the planet into a paradise.

He came back from his private reflections and said, "Laura Previn. A genetic engineer and a good one. Living in the Yenisey Region and believed to have been kidnapped. What makes her so important, Elias?"

"Tell me, Cap."

Weyburn was testing perhaps, seeing if Kennedy could find the answer shown by fragmented data. Weyburn could even have a desire for reassurance, the external evidence that he was still able to perform his function, but Kennedy didn't think it was as simple as that. Weyburn was a devious man.

He said flatly, "One thing, Elias. She isn't alone."

"No," admitted Weyburn. "She isn't."

"How many others?"

"Four." Weyburn looked at his hands. The blunt fingers were still and he wondered how much stress he would have to take before they trembled. When they did he would know that he was too old. "Four others, Cap. All at the top of their fields. All mysteriously vanished. In one case there was a fire, in another a flier crashed into the sea—I'll send you full details. Where is the *Mordain?*"

"On Luna. I caught the shuttle. You said to make certain I wasn't followed."

"With reason, Cap." Weyburn glanced around. They sat in an oasis of silence, only the soft susurration of birds disturbing the scented air. "Something's happening and I don't like the smell of it. Four experts, five with Laura Previn, all disappearing without a trace. Only luck and guts saved the *Shardorn.* If it had blown it would have been another mystery. And think of the cost of the operation, the trouble whoever was responsible went to."

"I've thought of it," said Kennedy. "I don't like the implications."

"You and me both." Weyburn scowled at a bird, not seeing the tiny, feathered shape. "When the computers showed something was wrong I had it determine the next five most likely victims. Laura Previn was one, which is why Commander Mbomoma was as close to the route of the *Shardorn* as he could get. Not that he could do any good, but it proved something. The kidnappings are all part of the same plan. Now who or what would want a group of experts? Want them enough to steal them, enough to make sure they couldn't be traced?"

"The galaxy is a big place, Elias."

"Too damned big. Too many little worlds with hungry rulers eager to grab a bigger slice of the cake. Ophrene, Zelgate, Instak, Xacamochis—the list is endless. Any one of them, offered the chance, would be willing to help destroy us if they thought they could get away with it. The Chambodians have tried it before and could be trying again. The Haddrach of Holme has been pressing, and even that bitch on Weingold seems to think we had something to do with the death of her officer on the *Shardorn*. She knows better, but any stick is good enough to beat Earth."

Kennedy made no comment; none was needed. Weyburn was simply telling the bald truth.

"Ambitious rulers I can understand. Cabals, hungry pressure-groups, deluded nobles, we've handled them all in our time. But madmen frighten me, Cap, and I don't mind admitting it. They're too unpredictable and too dangerous. And when you couple genius with insanity then I get really scared."

"You're saying something," said Kennedy. "What?"

"I'm talking about an old friend of yours. A ghost." From an inner pocket Weyburn produced a photograph. Holding it facedown he added, "Two things, Cap, which you should know. Schleheim managed to record some data on his log. One was a report that Corade wasn't what he seemed—a crewman grew suspicious—and we can take it as a fact that the saboteur was the man or thing inside. And something else. Schleheim caught a glimpse of the ship that attacked: big, limned with blue, a shimmering mist. And the thing had a mirror finish."

Kennedy tensed.

"And this." Weyburn handed him the photograph.

"Holtac. He was trying to tell us something when he died."

The details were painfully clear. The man's face was turned, the agony plain, blood red beneath his shoulder and torso. One arm was extended, the index finger stained crimson, more blood tracing a pattern on the deck. The twisted lines made no sense at first and then, as Kennedy turned the photograph, clicked into place: the design of a double helix.

. . . A symbol Kennedy had seen before—the insignia of Dr. Wei Kaifeng!

CHAPTER THREE

He sat in a throne-like chair at the end of a chamber hung with silken fabrics which glowed in the soft light of yellow lanterns. On his robes of rich maroon, ornamented with golden braid, the gemmed insignia of a double helix caught the light, reflected it so that the twisted coils seemed to move as they rested on his breast.

It was not the symbol which caught Laura Previn's eyes though, but the face above.

It was too cold, too remote, delicate skin drawn taut over prominent bone, the flesh seemingly transparent as if made of the finest china. The eyes were large, the emerald irises flecked with crimson, the orbs elongated and slanting upward beneath finely arched brows. The nose was thin, the mouth a cruel gash over a rounded chin, the ears small and neatly set against the domed skull.

"Laura Previn, a woman of distinction, you are an honored guest in my residence."

Like the face the voice was cold, the diction perfect.

"Guest?"

"The invitation was expressed in urgent terms perhaps, but you are a guest nevertheless." A thin hand lifted from where it rested on the arm of the chair. "Tsing, wine for the lady."

An underling came drifting from the shadows, squat, broad, his face a mask of stone. He deftly poured an emerald fluid from a decanter into a glass of engraved crystal and handed it to her with a bow.

Taking it, she wondered if all this was a dream: the

man—no, he had not been a man—the Mimic on the ship, the noise, the screams and confusion, then the flare of a Dione as he had burned open the door, lifting her, carrying her to the port, to the vessel beyond. The emergency suit had been ripped away and something like a gun leveled at her throat. As it fired she'd realized that it hadn't been a weapon but a hypogun to blast drugs through her skin and fat into the blood beneath.

And then, nothing. After a timeless period she had woken in a luxurious room dressed in a clinging gown of silver thread, the insignia of the double helix a scarlet flame over her left breast. The girl attending her had worn the same badge on her dull green tunic, its dullness matched by her eyes, her vacuous features.

And then she was brought to the tall man in the chair, the introduction, his name ringing as if a peal of bells.

She fought to control herself. The light was too soft, too deceptive; the designs on the silk hangings seemed to writhe at the edges of her vision, freezing only when she stared directly at them. The optical illusion gave an impression of closing spaces, of air which seemed like water.

She said harshly, "I was abducted. Men and women were wantonly slain. You will understand, Doctor, if I do not appreciate your sense of humor."

"You think I jest? Madam, you are mistaken. I am never other than serious. Tell me, had I asked you to come and join me, what would your answer have been?"

"I was busy. Too busy to spare time to indulge the whim of a—" She broke off, instinct warning her against finishing the sentence.

He said coldly, "Do you think I am mad?"

"Insanity is relative."

"True. It is a deviation from the norm, but what is that? Here, in this place, I decide what is normal. Accepting that, let us discuss the matter. What could I have offered you as an inducement to join me? Fame? Money? You have both. An enhanced reputation? You are at the top of your field. My need was great and the matter urgent, time could not be wasted in prolonged haggling.

There were other reasons which do not concern you. And what I need, I take."

Studying him, the glass unheeded in her hand, she knew it was a statement of fact and not an empty boast. And she also knew that nothing she could say, no persuasion she could use, would turn him from his intent.

"The wine," he urged. "You are not drinking your wine."

She looked at the emerald liquid.

"You think it drugged?" His tone almost held a dry humor. "You are a logical woman, Laura Previn. Why should I wait until now to instill compounds into your metabolism? What needed to be done is a thing of the past. Still you hesitate? Allow me to persuade you. Tsing!"

Like a drifting ghost the man came forward, took the glass and emptied it at a gulp. From the same decanter he poured fresh wine into another glass. The gesture meant nothing since the glass itself could have carried any poison, the man already primed with an antidote, yet the logic remained.

How could she know what may already have been done?

Only time could answer that question, but now there was something else she needed to know.

"Doctor, why was I brought here?"

"To work. To do all the things you have dreamed of doing but were prevented by social mores or stupid conventions." Rising, Kaifeng stepped toward her, his eyes aflame. "Experiments which could have taught you so much. Protoplasm changed beneath your direction into finer and more subtle shapes. Genetic combinations to open new doors of understanding. Here all those things are possible. That is what I offer you as your reward for cooperation—a laboratory in which you can pursue knowledge without the necessity of having to face artificial barriers. How often you must have been balked. . . . How well I understand."

"You?"

"In many places before—well, that is another matter

which does not concern you. Now let me show you the place where you will work, the things you must do."

"Must?"

"That is why you are here."

"And if I refuse?"

"You will not refuse."

She followed him, shaken by the flat conviction of the statement, hardly aware of Tsing as he took the glass, still untouched, from her hand. A panel slid open, the light beyond eye-bright after the yellowed gloom. A passage gave on to a small compartment with walls of chiseled stone. A ramp wound downward illuminated by the cold bluish glow of Kell lights.

From somewhere it seemed that drums began to beat, a steady, pulsing rhythm which quivered the very air until it throbbed with an ingrained sound at the edge of audible hearing. But it could not be drums. Instead it had to be the sound of machines, their vibrations transmitted through the rock and air of this place where she had found herself, an underground system of caverns perhaps, or chambers gouged from the side of a mountain.

And then she forgot all questions as she saw what awaited her.

It was a vast cavern filled with glowing light and set with an array of equipment finer than any she had ever seen: delicate apparatus with which to probe into the smallest particles of living tissue, a meson microscope, impulse field generators—machines to manipulate and engineer the elementary stuff of life itself.

And the place was busy. Men and women, dull-faced, dressed in the drab tunics she had seen before, moved with quiet purpose among vats and monitors, checking, testing, as much a part of the machinery as the metal and plastic itself.

"They are hands and eyes," said Kaifeng, guessing her thoughts. "Creatures of limited ability, lacking true dedication. They will be your assistants, an extension of your being, turning the flame of your genius into tangible results."

"Such as?"

For answer the doctor turned to the meson microscope and switched it on. The screen became alive, tiny flecks growing as he increased the magnification, resolving into a familiar pattern at which she stared with concentrated interest.

There were flashes like the darting of retinal images, the triple spirals of nucleotides, the morula. With a shock she recognized the unmistakable pattern of isovalhine, the genetic marker which warned of latent thyroid deficiency, a flaw in an otherwise perfect shape. It dissolved in a smear of brightness.

"A failure." Kaifeng switched off the instrument. "One of many, but perfection does not come easily. Yet it will come. Here you will create the ultimate in genetic design. Later we will talk about it. And now let me show you something else."

He directed her to a cabinet in which something moved. A mass of cells divided and kept dividing as she watched, the details blurred behind a shimmering skein of lambent blue fire.

"Notice," said Kaifeng. "Time within the cabinet does not move at the same pace as it does where we stand. There is an acceleration of approximately ten to one. A convenience which eases the tedium of waiting."

"A time-acceleration field!" It was the dream of every life-engineer. Ten experiments could be completed in the time it now took to do one. Ten channels could be explored at a time. More. "But who invented it? I have kept up with all the latest discoveries and there hasn't been a word. Nar Angik, perhaps? He was working on temporal displacement, but no, I remember now, he's dead. Who then?"

"Myself."

"You?"

"Do you think it so strange that I too am possessed of intelligence?"

"No, of course not." She looked at him with respect; whatever else he was, the doctor had genius. "It's just that I wonder why you didn't publish."

"For what reason? The adulation of fools? The acquisition of wealth? Small ambitions for small minds—I have a greater goal of which this is but a part." He glanced at the cabinet. The dividing cells had taken on shape and form, tiny embryos each within its own sac, growing even as he watched into further stages of development.

"A clone," she said, understanding. "All identical, all from the same parent cell. But why?"

"An experiment. You will pursue it. Now there is something you must learn."

He led the way from the laboratory to a room where a dull-faced, dully dressed man stood waiting. The man's eyes held the dumb appeal of a stricken animal.

"The one in charge of the party which took you from your ship," explained Kaifeng. "His orders were explicit, but he failed to carry them out to my satisfaction. He failed to obey. What should be his punishment?"

She thought it was a rhetorical question, or was he playing with her? Then she saw his face, his eyes, and felt a constriction of the stomach. The equipment in the laboratory had bemused her, scientific interest overwhelming her natural caution. Yet, even now, she could not believe that he would do more than administer a reprimand.

She slowly said, "Surely that depends on the nature of his error."

"Can there be degrees of failure?" Kaifeng shook his head. "There is only failure. And failure stems from the inability to obey. And I, here and everywhere, will be obeyed!"

"Master!" The man dropped to his knees, groveling. "Be merciful. The fault was not mine."

"A man lived who should have died," said Kaifeng coldly. "Things are known which should have remained hidden. You were in charge and there can be only one penalty. Tsing!"

He stepped forward, one spatulate hand reaching down, the fingers clamping to either side of the spine, lifting the screaming man so that his feet hung suspended from the floor.

"Pain," whispered Kaifeng. "The impacted nerves are filling his universe with nothing but pain. I would extend it so as to emphasize the lesson, but there is no time."

"Please!" Laura Previn felt sick at the spectacle. "Don't hurt him!"

"You are concerned, but why? What is this creature to you? Answer!"

She swallowed as she met his eyes. In some subtle way he had changed, his face bearing a feral satisfaction as if he gained pleasure from the agony of the hapless man, more pleasure from her futile defense.

"He is a man," she said. "A man."

"And what is that?" Contemptuously the doctor made a gesture and the screaming died, snapped off as if with a knife. Life was taken with a casual chop as Tsing snapped the man's neck with the stiffened edge of his free hand. "A set of bones, some tissue, blood, fat and skin—every animal has the same. The mind is what counts. The intelligence. Without it a man is just another beast. To be used and discarded when found at fault. Come now, you still have not drunk your wine."

They went back to the room with the silken hangings and the delusive yellow light. She picked up the glass with its emerald contents and stood looking at it as if she had never seen it before.

From his seat in the throne-like chair Kaifeng said evenly, "I suggest that you drink. It will aid you in what is to come."

"My work?"

"That also, but first comes the essential part of our relationship. You think of me, perhaps, as an equal. A colleague. If so you are mistaken. You are not and never will be my equal. And we are not colleagues. You were taken because I have a need of your skills. You will obey me in all things without question or hesitation. You will obey!"

"And if I don't? Will you kill me like you did that man?"

"No," he said softly, "I will not kill you. Instead you will suffer an eternity of hell, and soon now it will begin."

She looked at the glass, the wine it contained, wondering why she stood there with it in her hand instead of throwing it into his face, the cold, remote face with that expression she had seen before. Anticipation and a veil of gloating blurred the sharp delineations as if he had donned a mask of some thin but distorting crystal.

He was waiting, she realized, but for what? To see if the recent spectacle of death would shock her from what could only be a drugged diminution of her senses? To gauge the extent of the "lesson," her fear of the implicit warning?

He was an animal, she thought bleakly. A man with no sense of morals, no trace of restraint, and yet something more than a man: a warped genius who had given free rein to his consuming ambition. She stared at him, her head tilted, the yellow light bathing her figure and the silver gown with its hateful brand—hateful because it belonged to Kaifeng and he was not wholly human.

She could sense it, tell it with her trained eye, catching almost familiar snatches of recognition yet seeing them defy all her teaching. No truly human genetic pattern could have produced such a sense of inhumanity . . . the shape of the head, the eyes, the lines of the face. Why did he watch so intently? What did he expect?

And then it came.

A bath of sudden fire caught at her every nerve and laced the softly golden light with tides of red and black. The wineglass fell and she followed it, doubled, hearing strange noises, feeling the muscles tense at her throat, her mouth. She rolled, threshing, shrieking like a flayed beast left to burn in the sun.

It lasted for what seemed to be an eternity and then, as suddenly as it had come, the agony vanished to leave her gasping, crying, hands clawing at the thick carpet on the floor.

And, over the noise she was making, she heard the voice.

"Pain, the most efficient means of tuition which can be found. Tell a person something and strike him while you say it and he will never forget what he has heard. In ancient times children were taught that way and they learned fast and well. As you will learn."

"Please!" Her hair had come loose and hung over her sweat-dewed face, robbing her of years and making her appear young and pathetic. "What do you want of me?" Her voice rose, raw with remembered pain. "For God's sake, Kaifeng!"

"I am your master. Now and forever I am your master. You will remember that and address me accordingly. I will remind you again when the pain next strikes."

"Again!"

"To be learned well a lesson must be repeated. While unconscious you were injected with a compound of my own devising. Unless the antidote is administered at regular intervals you will suffer and finally die. Finally, but death will be long in coming. Disobey, displease me in any manner, and the antidote will be withheld for a period. I am sure you appreciate the position you are in."

He leaned forward in his chair as she slumped, knees lifting, hands clenched, heels thudding against the carpet, her mouth open and gaping, her eyes glazed with agony.

"Already you learn. Screaming does little to help, in fact it accentuates the pain. This is what you will do. From specimens I shall supply you will develop a method of accelerated production of clones. You will not make mistakes. You will work at the utmost speed. You will regularize the production so that it can be maintained with the minimum of supervision. You understand?"

"Yes! Yes, I understand!"

"You are slow to learn. How often do you wish to experience the repetition of what you suffer? A dozen times? A score? I must warn you that each attack will be more savage than the last. Answer properly."

"No! Please! For—" She crawled toward his chair. "Master! Help me!"

"You will obey?"

"Yes! Yes, Master! I will obey, but for God's sake—the pain!"

She turned into an animal as he watched, mewing, scrabbling blindly over the carpet, all culture and refinement forgotten in the constricting world of her personal hell.

Watching, leaning forward as if drinking her pain, Kaifeng said musingly, "You see, Tsing, how simple it is to bend a person to my will. All it requires is the applied force of pain and then, no matter how strong the opposing will, how adamant the initial refusal, inevitably all must break. Their own weakness defeats them and makes them tools of my will. Their skill, their intelligence, all are mine. And, as it is with this woman, so will it be with all."

"As you say, Master."

"Yes, Tsing, always as I say. The rule of nature teaches that the strong must rule. I am the strongest and therefore I will rule. Not one woman, not just a single world, but all. The entire galaxy. The universe."

He mused over his ambition in the golden flood of light while at his feet a woman sobbed and begged for release from pain.

CHAPTER FOUR

The feed to the multiple sprom cannon had checked out at less than perfect and though the technicians at Tycho Base had sworn it was operating at optimum efficiency Saratov wasn't satisfied. Now, crouched in the gun turret, he used micrometers and abrasive paste to rub the guides down to his own harshly defined tolerances. The military technicians might be content with optimum performance, but he wanted more than that. The *Mordain* had to be as perfect as skill and labor could achieve.

The micrometers weren't enough. Shifting his bulk, he set up a light-refraction meter and took a finding. A little more rubbing and it would be as good as he could get without a total dismantling. He squeezed his body into a space too small to take it, jerking as a noise echoed around him, a whining, wailing drone that tore at his nerves like a nail on slate.

He lifted his head and winced as it hit a projection—the last straw. His voice roared throughout the vessel.

"Veem! Stop that noise before I come down and wrap a wrench around your neck!"

The wailing died, replaced by a grieved voice.

"What's the matter, Penza? Don't you like music?"

"I like music, but I can't stand that racket. Why don't you make some coffee?"

The lesser of two evils. Saratov was convinced that Chemile could no more make good coffee than he could turn mud into radium, but at least it would keep him away from his new toy. An Ossenian flute needed expert handling and Chemile was no musician.

Another test and the big man was ready for a trial. Dropping into the chair, he hit the release and timed the speed of the large caliber self-propelled missiles from the hopper. A gain of almost 2 percent. Satisfied, he replaced the firing connections, reloaded the hoppers and replaced the housing. The guns would be ready when needed.

"That coffee ready yet, Veem?"

There was no answer. Saratov grimly replaced the tools in their racks and headed toward the galley. At first glance it was deserted, a thin thread of steam coming from the percolator, the Ossenian flute lying in clear view; he couldn't resist the temptation.

"Well, well," he said loudly. "So Veem's given up. I guess he couldn't face offering me that bilge he calls coffee. Still, maybe the flute will like it."

He picked it up in one big hand and reached for the percolator with the other, obviously going to drench the bag and ruin the reeds.

"No!" yelled a voice. "Penza, leave that flute alone!"

A section of the bulkhead seemed to dissolve and take on the shape of a man. Veem Chemile was tall and slender, with an upsweep of hair over a sloping brow and eyes like tiny gems in the smooth contours of his face. His skin was flecked with minute scraps of photosensitive tissue, giving him the chameleon-like ability to adopt the coloration of any background—a survival trait developed by his race on the savage world of his birth.

"Penza, put that flute down!"

Saratov chuckled as he held it beyond reach, one big hand pressed against Chemile's chest, pressing him back against the wall without effort. It was easy for him. Saratov was almost as wide as he was tall, with tempered muscle, bone and sinew disguising as fat. He had been born and reared on a world with three times normal Earth gravity.

"I should do it, Veem," he said seriously. "You can't

play it and you know it. If you don't want to drive us all crazy then get rid of the thing."

"You're jealous." Chemile twisted from beneath the relaxed hand and grabbed at the flute. "You couldn't play one if your life depended on it. Any more than you can make coffee. Once I get the full hang of it I might even be persuaded to entertain you while you tinker with the engines."

"Do that and I'll spray you with paint," rumbled the giant. "That'll cure your habit of sneaking around and trying to hide. What was the idea, anyway?"

"I was practicing. I can't afford to let my talent get rusty." Chemile lifted the flute to his lips, then quickly lowered it as Saratov made a grab. "All right. You don't have to break it. It cost me two hundred dollars from a crewman on MALACA 1."

"You were robbed."

"He needed the money. He said it cost him three times what I paid."

"You were still robbed." Saratov tasted the coffee, pursing his lips but making no comment.

"Good, isn't it?" Chemile smirked as he watched his friend. "Don't look so bad about it, Penza. We can't all be perfect. Be satisfied that you're a fairly good engineer and leave coffee-making to me."

Saratov took another sip. "I've tasted worse," he said after a moment's thought. "I can't say just when, but I have. I think it was on Eldarthara when they initiated me into the Alac tribe. They took muddy water and crushed a mess of insects into it. They also put in some rotten fish and a handful of moldering leaves. Now I come to think about it, it tasted just the same as this."

"You're lying!" Chemile was offended. "You haven't even the grace to admit I can make good coffee. You're nothing but a lump of overgrown lard."

"And you're a skinny freak." They grinned at each other, enjoying the banter, then Saratov said, more seriously, "What time did Cap say he would arrive?"

"Thirty minutes after the shuttle lands. He's going to pick up Jarl at the Reinhart Cultural Club."

The club lay to the south of the sprawling complex of Tycho, an appendage which had joined others at the extremity of the military base, the haunt of officers' wives, expatriates, people who for a hundred reasons had chosen to live away from Earth. Most of those attending the lecture were women, some of whom descended on Luden as he finished.

"Professor!" A gemmed matron held out her soft hand to rest it on his arm. "You were wonderful! To think that long before mankind ever learned how to make fire there was a race of intelligent creatures all over the galaxy. Do you think we shall ever find the Zheltyana?"

It was the dream of his life, but he didn't say so.

"I doubt if we ever will. All we have found so far are various artifacts which need not actually have belonged to the Ancient Race. They bear the Zheltyana Seal, so there must be a connection of some kind, but, as I explained in my lecture, we still lack any proof of what they looked like, where they came from and, above all, why they vanished."

"A mystery," she gushed. "Professor, when I listen to a man like you I feel so ignorant. And so inexperienced. To think that you have visited all those strange worlds and risked your life in the search for knowledge so that you could come here and tell us all about it. Weren't you ever afraid?"

"Often."

"Of monsters?"

The only monsters Luden feared were those around him, this woman and others of her kind, overdressed and bored females, too many with a calculating glint in their eyes.

Professor Jarl Luden would have been a catch at any dinner party.

His face was grave, his sparse body almost boyish in his flamboyant clothing: bright flashes of color on his flared pants, the collar and wrists of his blouse, the sash hugging his waist. Thick gray hair swept back from a high forehead. His eyes were a vivid blue, deep-set and alight with intelligence. His mouth was thin, down-curved as if he had tasted something not to his liking. As he looked over the heads of the thronging women his lips parted in a smile of relief at the sight of the man coming toward him.

"Cap! You timed it well." He grew serious at Kennedy's expression. "Trouble?"

"Yes. I'll tell you about it on the way to the *Mordain.*"

A pneumocar took them from the lower level of the auditorium, venting them at the base itself. Another carried them through the great airtight facility to the ship. Chemile turned from the radio as they entered, in his hands a sheaf of papers which had just come from the printer.

"From Weyburn, Cap. He said they were important."

"They are." Kennedy glanced to Saratov, who had joined them. "There is a possibility that Kaifeng is still alive."

"Alive?" The giant's boom held incredulity. "But Cap, that's impossible! We took care of him on Papan. Nothing could have lived through the blast of those torpedoes."

"Nothing is impossible, Penza," snapped Luden dryly. "It is only highly improbable. And Cap didn't say that Kaifeng was alive, he only said there was a possibility, perhaps remote, that he might be. I suggest that we study the evidence before making emotional statements based on limited knowledge. Some coffee, Veem?"

"I'll make it," said Saratov hastily. "But Kaifeng alive?" He shook his head as he went into the galley, shook it again as, later, he studied the photographs and other evidence. "A drawing, Cap. That's all we've really got. That and a glimpse of a silver vessel."

"A vessel with a mirror finish," corrected Luden. "One limned with blue radiance—Kaifeng's ship. We saw it in the cavern on Papan."

"And fired a full load of atomic torpedoes at the area," reminded the giant. "The entire valley was filled with molten slag, everything in the cavern was roasted, fused, burned or melted. Men, machines, everything."

"That's what we thought, Penza," said Kennedy. "But there was one other thing. Just before we fired there was a shimmer of blue, the glimpse of Kaifeng's vessel. It didn't register on the instruments and vanished even as we saw it. There was no time to make any kind of investigation—we were somewhat occupied when it appeared."

Shot, hurt, the *Mordain* demanded their full attention; the air was riven as atomic fire blasted the rock and soil below, erasing forever the menace which had appeared. At least they had thought so. Now it appeared they had been wrong.

"We must operate on the basis that Kaifeng is still alive. How doesn't matter for now." Kennedy riffled the reports Weyburn had sent, the list of missing persons. "Lars Horsen, mathematician, a genius in the application of hyperspatial equations. They thought he was killed in a fire at his house, but no positive evidence was ever found. Shign Baluka, electronics wizard. He vanished when his flier crashed into the sea. Marl Cayus, biochemical engineer, was assumed dead in an explosion at the laboratory on Weeple. Ghen Valdemar, cytologist, an apparent suicide though not a trace was found of his body." Pausing for a moment Kennedy added, "And Laura Previn, genetic engineer, who almost vanished with the ship she was on. Jarl?"

"A team, Cap," replied Luden instantly.

Saratov frowned. An expert engineer, he was a little slow when it came to intuition. "How do you make that out, Jarl?"

"Assuming that all these people were abducted by the same man or organization, there would have to be a reason for their actions. We know that it wasn't for purposes of ransom. Great care was taken to create blind alleys and give the impression that all had died. We know that Laura Previn was not killed on the *Shardorn*. Therefore she is probably still alive and it is highly probable the others are also."

"Held in one place," said Chemile. "Collected."

"Exactly, Veem." Luden nodded his approval. "Of course we cannot be certain and it is always unwise to speculate on the basis of scant evidence, but in this case the professions of those taken do fit into a recognizable pattern. All were at the summit of their class. Together they would make a formidable group of expert talent."

Saratov was stubborn. "For what purpose, Jarl?" What use could Kaifeng make of them?"

Kennedy said, "I think the answer lies in their talents, Penza. Each is a specialist in a certain field—mathematics, electronics, biochemistry, cytology, genetics. Obviously they weren't collected together to build, say, a ship. In that case there would be no use for a geneticist or a cytologist—what use would a specialist in the study of living cells be in such a case? But if you were interested in something else, the life-sciences, for example, then each would have a necessary function. Kaifeng, as we know, is a warped genius, but he is only one man. He personally can only do so much at a time. He must be investigating a new field of study and has taken those people to help him do it."

Kennedy could only guess at Kaifeng's diabolic purpose: the creation of monsters, perhaps, adapted forms of protoplasmic life. Maybe Kaifeng sought creatures to burrow far beneath the ground to wreck delicate installations, or others to carry vicious plagues, new viruses which modern medical science would be unable to combat—a thousand things.

. . . Death, drifting from the skies, walking around, rising from the very soil, carried on the very air itself. Leaving a swath of destruction on peaceful worlds, creating a chaos, a vacuum into which other, hungry races would throng.

And war would turn the galaxy into flame.

It would be inevitable. No matter what happened to Earth the MALACAs would remain unharmed. The tremendous concentrations of power stationed at scattered points in space, each with the armament sufficient to destroy suns, would take revenge. Dying, Earth would kill the innocent with the guilty, creating fear and guilt and triggering opposition.

And, when it was finally over and the shattered worlds lay helpless to resist, Kaifeng would come into his own.

Kennedy drew in his breath, shaking his head a little as if to clear his mental vision. Before him were scattered the papers Weyburn had sent, and he studied the photographs attached. Horsen was old, Baluka wizened, Cayus bland, his cheeks softly rounded; Valdemar was gaunt, but barely past middle age. Previn was the youngest of them all.

Kennedy lifted her file, looked at the face, the structure of bone beneath the skin. She must have been an attractive girl when younger; she was a beautiful woman now.

Luden cleared his throat with a dry rasping.

"It would seem that we have an almost insolvable problem, Cap. Where has Kaifeng taken those people? We can assume he has a base somewhere, probably an isolated world or planetoid. His ship was large, but it would still lack space for an extended project and the extensive apparatus required. The extrapolations made by the computers are hardly helpful."

"Because they are machines, Jarl, not men. They can only take facts and draw points of potential association." Kennedy dropped the woman's file and reached for others. They were the bare details of reports sent in by the undercover agents scattered on worlds throughout the known galaxy. "I had Weyburn get these. Reports on anything unusual, outside the normal pattern or of exceptional interest. And we have a clue. Laura Previn was on her way to Weingold. Someone must have invited her to address the convention. Kaifeng knew she was on her way. There could be a connection."

He quickly scanned the reports: on Heldhara there was a hitherto unknown interest in dueling, on Zenk a craving for celdeck had plunged the culture into an orgy of gambling, Bran had fostered a rebellion, Queedle was suffering from inflation, Jedkara from bands of masked ruffians, Raush from a minor epidemic.

"This could be it, Jarl." Kennedy handed Luden a report. "The centennial games on Weingold."

"An association, Cap," admitted Luden in his dryly precise tones. "The mate-games certainly have a bearing on the life-sciences and there seems to be nothing else aside from the epidemic on Raush. But the games are traditional, the epidemic is not."

Kennedy leaned back in his chair, eyes narrowed, his intuition taking over from the calculated thought processes of his forebrain. The instinctive leap joined isolated facts into a positive whole—the single great advantage a man had over a machine, no matter how complicated it was.

"Weingold," he decided. "We leave at once."

CHAPTER FIVE

Marita Xonig, Matriarch of Weingold, was in a foul temper. Three attendants had already felt the weight of her tongue and a fourth now cringed beneath the strident voice.

"Vanished? How could the fool have disappeared? The third so far. Are you positive?"

"Yes, madam."

"Get out! Send Yama in to me. Move, you slut!"

She rose from her padded chair and crossed the room to where salts and cordials stood on a small table. A servant could have fetched them to her, but she had had enough of servants, and besides, it was not wise to publicly reveal her dependence on medical aids. Servants talked and gossip ran like wildfire. Already they were saying that she was too old, that she could no longer command the respect of outworlders, that—and this was as yet barely hinted—it was time for another to take her place.

And, she thought bleakly, they could be right.

The stinging vapors rose around her withered face, caught at her nose, her eyes, clearing the one and filling the other with tears. She irritably blinked them away. Tears were a weakness no matter how induced, and no woman in her position could afford to be weak. After the games, when the bloodlines had been settled, then perhaps there would be time to relax. But now there was no time, and how could she be at ease with such disturbing news?

A knock and Yama entered. She was a tall, hard

woman, her face impassive, the green and black of her uniform relieved only by the silver insignia of her rank, a marshal of the guard. She might not be as good as Lina, thought the Matriarch, but Lina was dead, the association of years snapped by butchering pirates, and Yama had taken her place.

She said, "You sent for me, madam?"

"I did." Marita resumed her seat. Aside from the padding which her old bones demanded for comfort it was as Spartan as the rest of the room. The plain tiles and bare wood were softened only by a carpet and the ceiling was undecorated; the entire place was designed for function and not for ease. "I hear there has been another disappearance."

"Your information was premature, madam. As yet we have not been able to discover the whereabouts of the man or his mate, but—"

"But you're looking," snapped the Matriarch. Lina would have done more than look, she would have found, but what other woman could match her? "As you looked before. Three times now, isn't it?"

"Twice, madam."

"Without success."

"That is true." Yama Ukem met the baleful stare with equanimity. She had done her best; no woman could do more. "I cannot explain the mystery. The men had won, they and their mates had waited for settlement and then, when sent for, both had vanished."

"As they have vanished again." Marita sat, brooding, baffled by the unexpected. "They had no reason to go. They entered the games of their own free will. They had nothing to worry about. Just the use of their seed and, in return, a high reward. You must find them, Yama."

"Madam, I am doing my best."

"Which, apparently, isn't good enough. Double your security measures."

"That has already been done, madam."

"Then double them again." Damn the woman, was she being defiant? "Search the city, the planet if you have to.

People don't just vanish. Find them or lose your command!"

Yama Ukem carried that threat with her as she left the chamber, and she would pass it on in turn. She knew it would not do any good, however, for threats could not make a woman any more efficient or loyal. And her aides, as well as Yama herself, knew that the old hag couldn't last much longer. Her room stank of acrid vapors, soon she would be using drugs, already her temper was a byword. It was time to form new loyalties.

But for now, at least, Yama could tighten up things at the field.

It was thick with traffic, ships bearing hopeful contenders, tourists, those eager to witness the games. Most of the contenders would be quickly eliminated, the tourists would spend welcome money and a few of both would apply for residence. Some of them might even be accepted—some, but not many. Weingold was a carefully controlled world with a rigid discipline and high, rigorous standards that few outworlders could meet. Yet there was always the need for new blood, new gene patterns to expand the available pool.

There was an altercation beginning at one of the gates as Yama approached. A small group was passing through and a guard, a tough veteran, had taken exception to an obscenely fat man in loose garments.

"You!" She poked at him with a finger. "We don't need your kind on Weingold. Just take that bladder of lard back to where you came from."

Saratov scowled at the prodding finger. "Do that again and I'll teach you to be more polite."

"You?" Her laughter was derisive. "You, a man, teach *me?* Why, you fat fool, I could turn you into jelly with my bare hands."

"Try it."

Yama saw him move as the guard accepted the invitation, one hand reaching out to grip her harness, the arm lifting her squawking off the ground. Red-faced, the guard beat at the supporting arm.

"Well?" Saratov looked up at her, grinning. "When are you going to start?"

A rising chuckle came from the cluster of bystanders as the guard still continued to struggle. Women watched, their eyes pensive; men, soft and weakly muscled, laughed a little too loudly. A bad example, Yama felt. The guards should always maintain their dignity.

Stepping forward she snapped, "Put that woman down!"

Saratov's grin widened. "How's that? You want to join in?"

"Do as she says, Penza." Kennedy had seen the glint in the hard eyes, the thin compression of the lips. And he could tell from her insignia that she had the power to ban them from the planet—an inconvenience he wished to avoid.

Grunting, the guard adjusted her uniform.

"Madam, you saw what happened. I demand—"

"I saw what happened," said Yama flatly. "You provoked the man and you got what you asked for. You have no right to demand anything, certainly not from me. Now go to the next gate and resume your duties." To Saratov she said, "Are you a contender?"

"No, a tourist."

She felt dismay tinged with relief. A man with such strength might possibly win as a contender, but his squat appearance was not within the normal conception of beauty. Her eyes shifted toward the others. One was too old, the other too alien . . . the third?

"I am a contender," said Kennedy. "I must apologize for what happened, but each world has its different customs and my friend has a sense of humor. I am sure you will understand."

And, understanding, forgive. Yama felt a wry amusement at his subtlety, something else as she looked at his height, his features. This was a man all would be willing to accept. Had she been younger . . . but her right to breed had been lost when she first donned a uniform. Military families were not permitted since cabals could too easily be formed, loyalties dissipated.

"You are welcome on Weingold," she said and added, looking at Saratov, "It would be best to restrain your sense of humor. Had the guard shot, you would have had no grounds for complaint. In fact I think it would be best if you returned to your ship now. These people"—her head jerked toward the watching crowd—"would prove an embarrassment. When they have dispersed you may leave the field, but I suggest you avoid the guard you have already met."

Saratov shrugged. The delay was unimportant, he had only wanted to search the shops for subtle spices to improve his coffee. The others had different objectives.

"Veem, you go to the lecture hall where Laura Previn was to have given her address. Check to see if she was invited and if so by whom. You might have to search the records, but be careful."

"You don't have to tell me that, Cap. How shall I contact you?"

"By radio if I'm not at the *Mordain*. The local agent. Jarl and I are going there now."

Her name was Vivien Dreux and she lived in a house close to the center of town, in apartments above the offices of a news syndicate. She ostensibly owned the business, which covered a multitude of comings and goings—the perfect cover for an underground agent whose main task was to look and listen, relay messages and stand ready to give a helping hand in case of need.

She looked surprised as Kennedy gripped her wrist and dug the tip of his thumb against a nerve. The normally hidden tattoo of her secret identity appeared on the tender flesh.

"What's the matter, Cap, don't you trust me?" The question, she knew, was stupid. "Sorry, I guess you can't afford to trust anyone. Would you like some wine?"

He looked around as she crossed to the table where a sealed bottle and glasses stood. They were in an inner room in the residential part of the building and here, Kennedy knew, would be the equipment of Terran Control: the hybeam radio to keep her in touch, other things that would turn to molten ruin at the touch of an unauthorized hand. The room itself was like a vault, the repository of business secrets, the gossip and scandal picked up by a thousand free-lance operatives working for her syndicate.

"Here." She handed a glass to Luden, another to Kennedy. Lifting her own she said, "To peace!"

Drinking, Kennedy looked at her.

She was tall, the top of her head reaching to the edge of his jaw, her body lithely slim with swelling curves accentuated by the clinging fabric of her gown. Her hair was long and blonde, shimmering with hints of gold. It fell loosely about her face, framing the deep-set blue eyes; the lashes were long enough to rest on her cheeks when closed. Her mouth was wide and generous, the lips full, the lower betraying her sensuality. Her jaw was firm and her nose, slightly uptilted, gave her face a glowing vicacity.

He wondered how anyone so young could have reached her position.

"I was best fitted," she said when he'd flatly asked the question. "A native of Weingold who'd been educated on Earth. An agent here has to be a woman, you understand—men aren't taken seriously in this society—and I fitted the bill. When my—the other agent was killed in a crash—I simply took over."

Her mother, of course, even though she appeared reluctant to admit it. She had inherited both the syndicate and the agency, a convenient arrangement for all concerned.

Kennedy said, "Tell me about the games. Did you have any trouble getting me accepted as a contender?

"A little, but I've got influence and I used it. The preliminaries are over for this session. You could wait for the next, of course, but I guessed you didn't want to waste the time."

"You guessed right." Kennedy set down his empty glass. "What happens now?"

"The finals are tomorrow. We go to the stadium at dawn." She stared at him with frank appraisal, her eyes roving over his body, assessing the toughness she knew must be beneath the soft civilian clothing. "If you want to win, Cap, it isn't going to be easy. Some of those men are really tough and they mean to reach the top. They'd be willing to kill in order to do it."

This was accepted, even desired by the native culture. A hard, strong and ruthless man held genes of value; not for the sons he might sire, but for the daughters who would stem from his seed.

Luden said dryly, "We know about the games, my dear. A primitive method of selection, useful at one time, perhaps, but now surely unnecessary. However, that is not our concern. There is no doubt that the other winners have vanished?"

"None." She was emphatic. "I've checked and double checked. Three winners and their mates, all gone without a trace."

"All? Surely the last couple was well guarded?"

"They were and there's a mystery about it. The guards swore that nothing happened during their watch and yet, when the winner was summoned, they had gone."

Kennedy said, "Bribery?"

"No, Cap. One guard could have been reached, maybe two, but there were six, and all handpicked by Yama Ukem herself. She's the marshal of the guard and totally incorruptible. As I said, there's a mystery. Somehow those people were stolen away—God knows for what purpose."

"We can guess at that," said Kennedy grimly. "For raw material."

Luden nodded. "Obviously, Cap, you were correct in your assumption that Kaifeng would have an interest in the games. With the team he has at his disposal he must be interested in genetics and biological engineering. He would have need of selected specimens. But I wish that it wasn't necessary to place yourself in the position of bait. Too many things can go wrong."

"We have no choice, Jarl. If I win you can follow me in the *Mordain*. If not we can still keep watch, but with a handicap."

"I realize that, Cap, but I still don't like it. Kaifeng is utterly ruthless."

Vivien said, "Kaifeng?"

"The man we believe to be behind the disappearances." Kennedy looked sharply at her. "Have you heard the name before?"

"No, but I think you should tell me about him."

"Why?"

"Because, Cap, we're in this together."

"As members of Terran Control, perhaps," said Luden, "but—"

"As partners," she interrupted. "As a team."

The wine stood where she had left it. Picking up the bottle, she refilled their glasses, lifting her own to sip at the ruby liquid. The moistness accentuated the color of her lips, their sensuality.

"I thought you understood, Cap," she continued, "when you asked me to book you in as a contender. Everyone taking part in the games has to have a sponsor. Had you come early you would have seen this on the first day of the session. The men line up and are selected by interested women. Once she makes a choice, the woman considers the man to be her property. He is accepted legally as such. Should he win he automatically becomes a citizen under her domination. Don't forget that men have no standing on Weingold. They are regarded as second-class citizens, with all that implies. They can't even leave the planet without the permission of their accepted head."

"So?"

"You had to have a sponsor, Cap. Who else could I pick but myself?"

"So I'm you're property," said Kennedy, smiling. "Is that what you are telling me?"

"Only while you're on Weingold and only for the games. But if you win I shall have to be with you. It's the custom."

And a complication. Luden firmly protested, "I don't like this, Cap. Surely there must be some other way?"

"Is there, Vivien?"

"Not if you hope to set up as bait, Cap," she said

flatly. If you win you'll have to have someone with you. You won't even be allowed to enter the contest unless I'm there." The prospect seemed to please her. She added, "I'm sorry, but there it is. You'll have to take it or leave it."

"I'll take it," said Kennedy. "But I warn you now, it could cost you your life."

Hers and his both, but there was no choice. The danger had to be accepted if it could lead them to the base of Kaifeng's operations. Maybe he could even find a way of leaving the girl behind.

As she nodded he said, "Right, that's settled. Jarl, you know what has to be done. And now, Vivien, you'd better coach me as to what I should wear and how I should act. I've never been owned by a lovely young girl before."

"Do you think I'm lovely, Cap?"

"I've seen worse."

"Which is what they mean by a backhanded compliment, I suppose. Well, a girl can't have everything." She studied him carefully. "First you'd better change into something less expensive. None of the contenders who come here are rich. They hope to win the reward and live easy for the rest of their lives and don't mind losing their freedom to do it. And you'll have to attend me—the women like to show off their men, especially when they've reached the finals. It will give you a chance to study the opposition."

A good point. "And?"

"Let's discuss that when it comes," she said meaningfully. The tip of her tongue caressed her lower lip, a gesture accentuated by the expression in her eyes. The product of a matriarchy despite her education on Earth, she had absorbed local attitudes. On Weingold a woman was never slow in reaching for what she wanted—and it was obvious what that was.

As Luden left Kennedy said, "Well, I suppose we had better get on with it."

"Yes," she said thickly. "I suppose we had."

CHAPTER SIX

Dawn came with a flood of yellow light, bright streamers gilding the sky with a wash of scarlet and orange, warm light against the blue, the white of fleecy clouds. The stadium was already full, the sound of the crowd rising like the restless murmur of bees. It was a gay day, a holiday, one they were determined to enjoy. From her favored seat in the royal box Vivien waved as Kennedy turned to make the formal salute.

Arenas were all the same: a space in which men contended, tiers of seats from which the crowd watched, a special place for the favored; here sat the friends of the Matriarch, the women coupled to the final contenders, Marita Xonig herself.

Tiredly she lifted an arm and returned the salute.

Once she had reveled in the atmosphere of the games, but that had been a long time ago—a hundred years, during which she had changed from a comely young woman into a withered hag. In ten years, less even, she would be dead, her name forgotten. But for now she ruled.

From one of the women seated down to one side came a sharp protest.

"This is unfair! An extra man has joined the finals!"

"Yama?" The marshal leaned close, her voice a susurration in the Matriarch's ear. Marita nodded. "I understand. A special dispensation." She looked to where Vivien Dreux sat. She liked the young girl and felt inclined to help her. She looked radiant, as if she were in love or had found a lover. The two things, as the old woman knew, were not the same.

"Madam?" The woman who had protested turned to face the throne. "I protest."

"Noted and dismissed. If the mistress of ceremonies has allowed the man to compete then he has the right."

"But—"

"You tire me. If he can win over the best then he will prove himself to be the better man. Let the contest begin!"

There were no weapons. They were here to determine strength and physical fitness, not trained skill with lethal devices. The morning passed in trials of running, jumping, tossing heavy weights, swarming over obstacles. The variety of strenuous pursuits tested each man against every other, those proving themselves inferior being sent from the arena.

Finally only four contenders were left. Kennedy studied the others. One was breathing too harshly—pressed, he would collapse. Another was sweating too profusely, his eyes betraying the strain of his labors. The third was a giant of a man, richly muscled, apparently unaffected by the previous exertions.

"Hurdles." The mistress of ceremonies was a bustling woman with a voice as deep as a man's. "All together, the last two to be eliminated. Take your places. Set? Go!"

This was a test of agility as well as brute strength. Kennedy raced down the curving track, rose at the first hurdle, ran again as his feet hit the dirt, rose again at the next barrier. At the tenth the man who had breathed too hard tumbled as his foot caught on the top bar. At the twenty-second the man who had sweated too profusely stumbled and was out of the race. Kennedy immediately slowed, allowing the giant to draw well ahead.

The man was strong, trained, a dedicated athlete. Kennedy knew there was no point in wasting energy to claim an unessential victory.

"The final contest," said the mistress of ceremonies. "One of you will win. The one who can throw the ball the farthest. The best two out of three."

Kennedy looked at where the balls lay, heavy spheres of stone and lead, each weighing fifty pounds. Bodo, the remaining contender, looked at him, grinning as he saw Kennedy's look of concern.

"Too heavy for you, friend? Here, let me show you how it's done."

He swaggered forward, picked up one of the balls and hefted it on the palm of his right hand. Turning his back toward the length of the arena he paused a moment, tensed, then turned and casually flung the heavy ball. He grinned as it came to rest.

"There. Now see if you can beat that."

Kennedy looked at it, shaking his head as he picked up a ball, thinning his lips as he tensed, then turned and threw. His ball landed two feet past the other—a win.

Bodo grunted as he picked up his second ball. This time there was nothing casual about the way he stood, the muscles bulging beneath his skin, air rasping as it gushed through his nostrils. He stood still for a moment before turning in an explosion of energy like a released spring. The ball soared high and far to land well down the stretch of sand.

Kennedy knew he could not hope to beat that throw easily.

But he tried, apparently.

He stooped, lifted the ball and stood obviously summoning every fragment of his strength. He remained tense for a long moment as if gearing himself to the final, supreme effort, then turned and threw the ball, staggering a little as if exhausted by the effort.

It landed barely a foot in front of his previous throw—yards behind his opponent's second mark.

"One all." The woman looked at the sun. It was past noon and the Matriarch would be getting impatient. "The next throw decides who is to be the winner."

Bodo picked up his last ball. He saw the woman who had selected him smiling as she stared down from the box. He smiled back, already tasting the rich, idle life ahead. Conceit made him overconfident. Kennedy had obviously made the best throw he was capable of, a throw Bodo could easily beat by a yard. There was no need to exert himself to the full and risk a torn muscle.

He casually tossed the ball.

Kennedy tensed himself as his turn came, not as he had done before in pretense, but this time with calculated intent. His first throw had been made simply to beat the other man's, his second to give the impression that he had done his best. Bodo had fallen into the trap. Instead of exerting himself to the full and making his third throw impossible to beat, he had restrained himself—a mistake, as Kennedy proved.

A shout rose from the crowd as his ball landed a good yard beyond the other's.

Bodo stared, incredulous, then turned, his face contorted with rage.

"You lied. You tricked me. You cheated."

Kennedy snapped, "You lost."

"I wouldn't have lost. I had you beaten easily. If you hadn't—" His anger rose beyond control. With a rush he crossed the distance between them, hands lifted to grip and tear.

Kennedy dodged, dropped to one knee, caught at a passing ankle and, straightening, heaved.

Bodo, caught off balance, fell to the sand, then rolled to spring to his feet with murder in his eyes. Again he advanced, more cautious now, adopting the stance of a wrestler, his hands moving shields.

In the box Yama Ukem stooped and whispered, "Madam, shall I call a halt?"

"No!" For the first time during the games Marita felt herself come fully alive. She leaned forward, eyes devouring the spectacle below. Two men locked hand to hand in savage combat—thus had it been in the old days. "Let them fight to the death if they must. Let the best man win."

Blinded, perhaps maimed, the Matriarch considered, but what did eyes matter or a crippled body? Only the genes were important and they would not be harmed.

Her senses swam, then cleared as if to the touch of her noxious vapors.

Kennedy was backing away.

He moved slowly, carefully, each naked foot scraping the sand in search of obstacles, anything that might cause him to trip. Before him Bodo advanced, a man turned into an animal by rage, but with a man's brain and skills proved in a dozen arenas. His stance told of that: the set of his head into his shoulders, the chin lowered to protect the throat, the hands stiffened, weaving, blades of bone and muscle ready to stab or chop.

The crowd sucked in its breath.

It was waiting to see the flurry of action, the blows, the blood, hear the snap of bone, the screams torn by pain from ruptured tissues.

Kennedy moved.

He jerked to one side and back, sand flying up from his kicking foot, sharp grains spattering over Bodo's snarling face, the glaring eyes. He moved again, running, turning as he reached the giant frame, his hand lifting to slash down like a blunted ax, the edge slamming against the mammoth biceps with its bunched muscle.

Such a blow would have broken the arm of a normal man.

Bodo felt it, felt the numbness induced by the impacted nerve, the pain. It added to his rage and robbed him of caution. Kennedy was fast, lithe, a rapier against a cutlass. As Bodo's thick arms opened he dived in, the tips of his fingers spearing the solar plexus, ramming hard against knotted muscle. Bodo could have ridden the blow, but not with the smash to the head which followed it, or the knee which drove into his groin. The three-pronged attack sent him reeling, blood masking his mouth and chin from his broken nose, doubled and retching, helpless to defend himself.

Kennedy could have killed him then. Instead he backed away, looking at the mistress of ceremonies.

"Enough?"

"Enough," she admitted reluctantly. "You are the winner."

The roar of the crowd was like thunder.

"You were lucky," said Vivien as she toyed with a heap of fruit and cream. "Suppose he had called your bluff and really tried to win that last throw?"

"I would have done the same as he did," said Kennedy blandly. "Accused him of cheating and challenged him to a fight."

"And you would have won it too." She stabbed at her sweet. "Cap, you are a very special kind of man."

Kennedy leaned back in his chair, not answering, knowing that no comment was expected. The afternoon had been hectic, but now the ceremonies were almost over, the speeches made, the acclaim of the crowd but a memory. The Matriarch had presented him with a badge and chain which would gain him some respect if he stayed on the planet. She expected him to stay and he hadn't disillusioned her. But now, with the banquet drawing to a close and night already fallen, he began to feel tense.

Tonight, if the pattern was followed, he would be snatched from the room set aside in the palace . . . abducted and taken, he hoped, to Kaifeng.

He said quietly, "Vivien, listen to me. When we leave I want you to go home. Make some excuse but don't join me in the palace. You understand?"

"No, Cap."

"It's simple. I want—"

"I know what you want, Cap, but it isn't what you're going to get. You're trying to protect me, but it isn't possible. See those guards? They are going to escort us. Once we're in the room they are going to protect us. Ten of them. Yama Ukem must be getting anxious."

"And you?"

She took a mouthful of fruit, chewed and swallowed.

"I'm uneasy," she admitted. "But I'm not afraid. Not while I'm with you."

"I should have gone back to the *Mordain* last night."

"Was it that bad?" Smiling, she read the answer in his eyes. "You had to live a part, Cap, and you still have to live it. We daren't do anything unusual or out of pattern. Now relax, I knew what I was letting myself in for. It's all part of the job."

She obviously found her part exciting and had taken advantage of her position. Kennedy had allowed her to take the advantage, knowing as well as she did that there really was no choice. Besides, Kennedy reflected, in the battle he fought personal considerations came last. If she had to die to maintain the pretense, then he would let her die. The worlds of Terran Control could not be risked for the sake of a woman. He had tried to tell her that in the silent darkness, only to feel the touch of her fingers on his lips.

"I know, Cap, darling. I know. But for now let me dream."

He had dreamed too, lying in the softly warm circle of her arms, tranquil in an oasis of content far from the exigencies of the moment, the dangers to come. He had lain like that until the cold light of pre-dawn had washed across the sky, lightening the window to reveal the tumbled glory of her hair at his side.

She hoped it would happen again and he hoped it would not . . . for if another dawn found them together it would mean the plan had failed.

CHAPTER SEVEN

The guards were alert, the marshal officious. Yama Ukem stepped into the room from the passage and tested each window, checked the bathroom, the furnishings, even the wide double bed.

Kennedy said, "Is this the same room the others had?"

"No. That was on a lower floor. This is as high as we can get in this part of the palace."

"It will do nicely," said Vivien. "Thank you, Yama."

"If there is anything you want just ask the guard outside. There are four in the passage and three in the rooms at either side."

"And on the stairway leading up? The elevator?"

"A separate contingent at the foot of the stairs. The elevator will be put out of operational order." Yama Ukem looked at Kennedy with a grudging respect. "I would not have thought you would take such an interest."

"A comment, no more. I am sure you know the best steps to take to ensure our protection."

"Rumors," she said. "Nothing happened to the others and nothing will happen to you. If you've heard tales they are just rumors." She stiffened, saluting. "May fertility attend you."

Vivien shook her head as the door closed behind the marshal.

"A liar," she said. "I didn't know she had it in her. How stupid does she think I must be?"

"Perhaps she was only trying to be kind." Kennedy crossed to the window and tugged at the pane. It remained closed. Through it he could see a sheer drop to a courtyard below. Twisting his head to look upward, he saw an outflung eave. It would be possible for someone to swing down from it over the sloping roof above and cut open the window without a sound—but they certainly couldn't do it without leaving a trace. "Were the other rooms just like this one?"

"I don't know" Vivien came toward him, halting at his side. "I guess the first one had windows which could open. The last was on the lower floor and there could be a secret panel somewhere. The palace is very old and no one knows quite what it contains." She paused for a moment then added softly, "But what does it matter, Cap? The whole idea is for us to be taken, isn't it?"

"For me to be taken."

"But you agreed—"

"To keep up the pretense." He turned to look at her. "But I'm telling you now that if there's any chance of keeping you away from Kaifeng I'll take it."

She relaxed on the bed as he searched the room, lying back as he tapped the paneling and checked the floor and ceiling—yielding, she knew, to the basic instincts of survival, the need to know an enemy even if the intention was to surrender.

As he finished she said, "Cap, what's so terrible about Kaifeng? You've dealt with madmen before. I know you said he's a warped genius, but what real harm can one man do?"

"Destroy a world," said Kennedy flatly. "If he is a carrier of some infectious plague and is allowed to run loose. Never make the mistake of underestimating your enemy. Dr. Wei Kaifeng is not an ordinary man. He is brilliant, originally a native of Phuket. He graduated from the Szamao Institute and took postgraduate studies at the Kalarch Foundation. He has a dozen accepted degrees in a range of sciences and is a master at organization. I regard him as the most dangerous man to have ever lived, especially because of what happened to him on Sheol."

"Sheol?" She frowned. "I've heard of that planet, but you said he was a native of Phuket."

"I said that he was originally a native of Phuket—but you'd never guess it to look at him now. I have a file on him at the *Mordain*. I sealed it. Now it's open again."

"You thought you'd killed him," she said with quick understanding. "That he was safely dead."

"Yes."

"And he isn't. Are you sure?"

"No," Kennedy confessed. "I'm not sure, but I'm as certain as any man can be without seeing the actual proof of Kaifeng himself in the flesh. And when I do—"

"You'll kill him," she said. "Cap, I don't like your looking like that. Your face—it changed. I hope to God you never look at me with that expression. Sheol," she mused. "I remember now. Isn't that the home of the Kriad?"

"It is."

"And they do things to people. Cure them?"

"Sometimes." He felt the tiny muscles knot at the edge of his jaw. "And always for a price. Kaifeng paid it and they turned him into something other than human. Now go to sleep."

"Sleep?"

Later, when she breathed deeply, easily, her hair a tumbled mass of gold, her wide, generous mouth lax with satiation, he eased himself upright from her arms. Beyond the window all was dark, even the softly luminescent lanterns in the courtyard below had been extinguished. There was no moon, only faint starlight filtering through the gloom, and no sound aside from the muted creak and rustle from fabric and harnesses as the guards moved at their posts beyond the door.

It was, he guessed, at least two hours past midnight. Dawn would come in another four. If Kaifeng was going to act it would have to be soon.

He dressed quietly in the darkness, the soft fabrics cool to his skin, a blouse of dull purple laced with black, black pants laced with purple, a wide belt of saffron, shoes to match the belt. He tensed, listening. The small sounds from beyond the door had ceased.

Kennedy glanced at the girl—she hadn't moved. He quickly thrust his right hand under his blouse, feeling the tiny nodule beneath the skin in the region of his heart, pressing it to activate the tiny hybeam transmitter buried in his flesh.

High above, in its stationary orbit about the planet, the *Mordain* would pick up the signal and follow it wherever it would go. Once the bait had been taken that very bait would lead the way to Kaifeng's base.

On the bed the girl stirred and murmured, "Cap, my darling. Cap."

He stepped forward, the fingers of his right hand hovering over her throat, the pulsing carotid arteries. If she woke he would press them, blocking the flow of blood to the brain and bringing immediate unconsciousness. He relaxed as she stirred again then settled, breathing deeply, lost in the figment of a pleasant dream.

He gently opened the door. The light in the passage was a soft lavender effulgence in which shapes stood blurred as if seen under water. The guard facing him stood with unblinking immobility, a statue of flesh and blood. Her harness polished, the weapons at her belt reflected a dull sheen. He stepped toward her, noting her eyes, the pupils contracted to pinpoints. The eyes did not move or blink as he passed his hand before her face. The other guards stood to either side, also frozen in apparent paralysis.

The air was heavy, still, filled with a brooding menace.

The guards had been drugged, thrown into stasis by some means, perhaps an electronic beam or a gas. They would recover without ever having been aware of what had happened. Those responsible must be close.

Turning, he saw them almost at once.

They seemed to appear from the very air, shapes with the appearance of men, oddly blurred around the edges, amorphous figures which baffled the eye. He struck at one and felt the gritty smoothness of a peculiar fabric and then they were on him, one lifting a squat tube toward his face.

Kennedy relaxed and held his breath.

The vapor stung like ice, chilling and numbing his face. Hands were all over him as he slumped, the rustle of fabric loud in his ears. Something covered him with enveloping folds, binding his arms, his legs, blinding his vision. He heard the quick mutter of voices, the words indistinguishable, then the fabric was plucked from his face.

"Again!" whispered a voice. "Quickly!"

They had sensed that he was still conscious. The squat tube appeared again, venting another gush of chilling vapor, trapped this time by the fabric which again covered his face. To resist was useless; the gas was already permeating his skin and bringing a growing numbness. To struggle would only delay the inevitable and, worse, arouse the suspicion that he was not what he seemed. He inhaled deliberately.

And fell instantly into an ebony darkness.

On the *Mordain* Luden said sharply, "Stand by, Veem. Cap is signaling."

Chemile was at the controls. Saratov joined the professor in the laboratory, facing ranked dials and screens. On one of them, superimposed on an image of the city below, a tiny point of light winked in a rapidly changing pattern.

"The signal." Saratov emptied his chest with a gusting sigh. "Cap must have just activated the beacon. You're sure it's the right one, Jarl?"

"There is no mistake, Penza. The pattern is unmistakable." Luden was patient as he explained the obvious. He understood the giant's concern. Saratov had made the instrument and Kennedy was trusting it with his life. "No sign of movement as yet," he murmured. "I'll try increasing the magnification."

The image on the screen expanded, wavering a little as other points of light, blurred and erratic, appeared at various points. These others were electronic faults from badly maintained apparatus which, by coincidence, were broadcasting on an overlapping band. Against them the original signal showed strong and clear.

"Still no sign of movement." Luden thrust his face closer to the screen. "Cap could be simply waiting or—No. Wait."

"It's moving, Jarl!"

"One-tenth of an inch," agreed Luden. "Which at this scale means he's moved at least ten feet." Calibration lines appeared on the screen as he touched a control, a sharply-defined grid of luminous emerald. "Twenty feet," he said. "Thirty."

"They've got him," rumbled Saratov. "They must be taking him out of the palace."

From a speaker Chemile said, "What's happening, Jarl? Have they got Cap?"

"Switch on your monitor. See it?"

"Just about."

"I'll amplify." The moving point of light blazed with added brilliance. "Now?"

"Got it, Jarl." Chemile sounded puzzled. "But they're heading north, away from the field."

. . . To where a small ship was hidden in a gulley masked with thick vegetation. The vessel rose silently into the darkness, unlit, lifting through the atmosphere in direct contravention of all local laws.

As it reached space Luden said, "Follow it, Veem. Don't get too close—we don't want to be spotted—but don't lose it."

"I know what to do, Jarl."

"You'd better. If you make a mess of it I'll ram that flute of yours down your throat," rumbled Saratov.

"If I do, I'll help you." Chemile was confident of his skill, as were the others. "I'll even drink some of that swill you call coffee. All right if I just follow the vessel, Jarl? I can keep a better distance."

"A moment, Veem." Luden checked the glowing point of pulsing light, dimmer now despite the maximum amplification. Around it showed a soft fuzz of yellow, the emitted radiation of the vessel itself, the fuzz deepening as the ship reached plus-C velocity. It was moving fast and increasing its velocity, but the *Mordain* was the fastest vessel in space. "All right, Veem, do as you say. I'll run a continual monitor on Cap while you track the vessel. Now, Penza, how about some coffee?"

Time dragged as they settled into a routine, one resting as the others watched, brief snatches of sleep interspersed by long periods of concentration. Luden was about to relieve Chemile when the alarm rang with strident urgency.

"Veem?"

"Nothing." Chemile waved at the screens, empty but for the cold light of stars, the red fleck of the ship they were following. "Check the Larvic-Shaw."

The screen of the detector showed a mass of writhing lines, the central node very close. Luden checked it and returned to the control panel.

"Something's out there," he said flatly. "A mass of some kind and very close."

"Invisible, Jarl?"

"A simple matter of a rotational field which moves all radiation in a hundred and eighty degree arc. We could be looking directly at it and see only the region of space beyond, but the very rotation which makes it invisible to our eyes creates a spatial disturbance which registers on the Larvic-Shaw." Luden thinned his lips, watching. "There it is!"

It appeared from nowhere, occupying an apparently empty region of space, a huge, glimmering mass oddly shaped and wreathed in a glowing aura of bluish light. It seemed to vanish again as the light died, the mirror-finish of its hull reflecting the stars and creating the illusion of emptiness.

They had all seen that ship before—Kaifeng's!

Saratov took his place at the guns as Luden returned to the laboratory. His hands itched to aim the weapons and press the releases, to fire the heavy-duty Dione, spray the area with self-propelled missiles and launch the sleek, deadly torpedoes with their atomic warheads; but he knew better than to yield to temptation. Destroying the enigmatic vessel would mean damaging the one now close to its glimmering hull, the ship which held Kennedy.

He could do nothing but watch and wait.

"They're making a transfer," said Chemile. "Jarl?"

"I'm monitoring, Veem." Despite the strain Luden's voice was calm. "You are correct. Cap is being moved from the small ship. We might have expected it."

"Why, Jarl?"

Kaifeng would want his base kept secret. The fewer who know where it is the greater the chance of maintaining that secrecy." Luden frowned as he watched his screens. The pulsating signal point was fading, dying as the blue radiance again limned the glittering hull. "Veem! Be ready! The ship is about to move!"

It flickered and was suddenly distant. The engines of the *Mordain* hummed as Chemile fed power to the drive. Small vibrations began to quiver the metal, ghost noises caused by the savage increase in acceleration, the mounting velocity.

For a second the blue-limned radiance came closer and then, with shocking abruptness, it was gone.

"Jarl!"

"Maintain course, Veem!" Luden hit switches and stared at the monitor screen of the Larvic-Shaw detector. "Three degrees left and five up. Full power!"

"Got it, Jarl."

"Penza! Get to the engines. We need all the power we can get." Luden thinned his lips as he read the message of the writhing lines. "We're falling back. Faster, Veem!"

It was hopeless. Even as he watched, the convoluted mesh of lines began to straighten, the node dissolving, the screen clearing to show only the normal pattern of space.

Kaifeng's vessel had gone, vanished—and Kennedy had gone with it.

CHAPTER EIGHT

He woke up in a room that smelled of roses. The ceiling was low, the stone floor softened by a rug graced with abstract designs. One wall was all of iron bars, the box of a lock holding fast a narrow door. The cold blue light stemmed from a single Kell.

Kennedy lay looking at it, not moving, not even turning his eyes after the first quick glance. He felt a little light-headed as if from an extended lack of food, but otherwise completely fit. The slight giddiness would pass, he knew, and there was no point in action without purpose. For now it was sufficient to rest, to waken the full resources of body and mind, to prepare himself for what was to come.

The vapor had thrown him into a form of metabolic stasis, he guessed. Unconscious he had been carried from the palace to a ship and from Weingold to—where?

The Kell gave part of the answer. It was a translucent bulb containing a pinch of radioactive isotope; the radiation caused the compound covering the interior of the bulb to shine with a steady fluorescence. Such bulbs were used as emergency lighting on all ships. Mines had them, underground caverns, disused passages, the hovels of the poor. Needing no attention, they would last for years.

He was somewhere underground then, not on a ship—he could sense that with an instinctive conviction—but in a chamber gouged from the living stone of Kaifeng's base.

He closed his eyes as sounds came from beyond the locked grille, the shuffle of footsteps, a voice, a murmured answer.

"Is this the last of the specimens?"

"My lady, I do not know. I only obey the will of the master."

"As do we all." The voice was tired, bitter. "Well, let me see him."

Kennedy heard the click of a lock, the slight grate of hinges as the narrow door opened. Fingers rested on his forehead, moved to the pulse in his throat, dropped lower to grip the upper edge of the single cover. A jerk and it fell from his naked body.

"Good musculature, excellent skin tone, very little fat." The voice was dispassionate, that of a person commenting on a prime animal. "Fine bone structure and superb proportions. Physically, at least, he is the best yet."

"You will waken him?"

"Of course. Later."

"Will you need aid, my lady?"

"No. Leave me. Wait outside." As footsteps moved away her fingers rested lightly on Kennedy's eyes. Quietly she said, "You are awake. Open your eyes."

She had changed. Her hair was streaked with gray, her eyes meshed with lines at the corners, slightly pouched beneath. The skin of her cheeks and throat was creped, the line of the jaw softened, the lips thinned. Here was a woman older than the one whose likeness he had memorized, but certain things were unmistakable, such as the bone structure.

He spoke softly. "Laura Previn?"

Her eyes widened, one hand lifting to her throat. "You know me?"

"I know of you. What has happened to you?"

"This?" She touched her hair, her eyes. "Magic," she said bitterly. "The magic of Kaifeng."

"He is here? You've seen him?"

"I've seen him." She made a gesture as if at a loathsome memory. "Too often and for too long."

"Describe him." Kennedy listened, his face growing

hard. There had been a bare possibility that only the name and insignia had survived; now he knew that the man himself had escaped destruction. "Where is he now?"

"I don't know. He could be anywhere—he doesn't take me into his confidence. And you? Who are you?"

"A friend."

"I've never seen you before in my life."

"Does that make me your enemy?" Kennedy met her eyes, saw the questions there, the ones he dared not answer. "Let us just say that a group of people were concerned at your disappearance and asked me to find you. I was able to win the games on Weingold and here I am."

"People," she said. "Which people? Why should they consider me to be so important?"

"You and certain others. Horsen, Baluka, Cayus, Valdemar. Are they here? Have you seen them?"

"Yes." She turned, glancing back to the bars of the cell, the passage beyond.

Kennedy said quickly, "Tell me, how free are you? Can you move at will about this base?"

"No. Only within a certain sector."

"Where are we? Do you know?"

He frowned as she shook her head. Like himself, she would have been rendered unconscious, stripped and searched, told nothing of importance. Yet Kennedy knew she was an intelligent woman. She must have learned something. And what had made her so old?

She said, "We can't stay here. The guard will be getting suspicious. I was to have wakened you and given you preliminary tests: elementary responses to selected stimuli to ensure that your mental coordination remains unimpaired. Other tests will be made in the laboratory. There is a robe beneath the bed. Put it on and follow me."

"And?"

"No questions," she said. "Not here, not now, please!"

Rising, he slipped on the thin robe of smooth gray fabric with the double helix in black. Knotting it with a braided cord, he followed the woman from the cell. The guard fell into step behind them as Laura Previn led the way down the passage, the stone roof set with Kells. The guard was a broad man, flat-faced, his eyes expressionless. He was apparently unarmed, but wore a wide belt of some shining material, the ebony band adorned with an oblong box-like attachment where the buckle should have been. The surface of the box was centered with a dull boss. The insignia of the double helix was traced in yellow on the left breast of the man's drab tunic.

Red for the woman, noted Kennedy, yellow for the guard, black for himself, the various colors signifying rank, perhaps. The guard, he noticed, kept one hand tucked in the belt, his thumb resting on the upper edge of the box-like buckle.

Kennedy asked softly, "What would happen if I attacked that man?"

"Don't try it."

"I asked what would happen."

"You'd suffer," she said. "And in this limited space so would I. Pain, disgusting, degrading, unbearable." She spoke with the bitterness of personal experience.

"More of Kaifeng's magic?"

"You could call it that. An electronic whip which convulses every muscle into searing cramps. Effective at short range. Be silent now."

Kennedy had no intention of obeying that command. He was, superficially, the best of the games, aggressive, arrogant, a man who would naturally be pugnacious at what had happened.

He said loudly, "I don't go along with this. I want to know what's happened. Why am I here? Who is this character you spoke of?"

"Be silent!"

"Like hell I will!" He halted, glaring. "Listen, you, I want some answers. If I don't get them I'll break a few heads."

"You are being foolish."

"Maybe, but I'm not going to be pushed around. Take me to the boss. I want to know what all this is about."

"Proceed, my lady." The guard had moved to put his

back against the wall of the passage. As the woman walked quickly away he took two steps sidewise to face Kennedy. "You will not question. You will obey. That is the will of the master."

"To hell with the master!"

Kennedy saw the tension of the guard's thumb and lunged forward as it thrust a button home. Pain caught him in mid-air, doubling him with searing agony, causing him to roll, sweating, on the ground. The pain lasted for a long agonizing moment and then vanished as quickly as it had come, but he did not move, lying where he had fallen, moaning, lips contracted to show his teeth in a rictus of pain.

The woman had told the truth.

The agony had been intense, but he had learned.

"Rise," snapped the guard. "Quickly." He stepped back as Kennedy rose slowly to his feet. His muscles felt sore, little bunches of tissue aching as if at prolonged strain. "Now move. Hesitate and you will suffer again."

They continued through thick doors to the laboratory, a place with acrid smells, benches, a long couch to which Kennedy was strapped. Assistants moved deftly at their work; the guard, gestured aside, took up a station beside the door out of the way and safely out of earshot.

Kennedy looked around as the woman busied herself with machines.

The place to which he had been taken was, he decided, only a part of the laboratory proper. To one side rose a wall limned with flickering blue radiance. As he watched a door opened in it and a man came through the opening.

He was old. His tunic hung on skeletal shoulders and his limbs were like sticks. His eyes were red, the lower lids sagging, his cheeks deeply lined. Thin hair clung to a balding forehead and his hands trembled as if with ague.

He nodded to Laura Previn, glanced once at Kennedy, then moved on to vanish through another door.

"Lars Horsen," she said quietly. "The others are almost as bad."

"How?"

"I told you, the magic of Kaifeng." She attached electrodes to various parts of his body. "A time-acceleration field. You can see the blue glow—stay away from it if you value your life."

"Will I be given the chance?"

"I don't know." She threw switches and frowned as she read the result on the panel of the machine standing beside the couch. "In fact I don't know anything. How can I be sure that you are what you claim to be? Kaifeng is a sadist. It would be like him to trap me."

"Into what?" Kennedy shrugged as she didn't answer. "I came to find out what happened to you and the others. Obviously you're working for Kaifeng. Are you going to tell him about me?"

"It might be wise."

"In which case you'll lose any chance you may ever have of getting away from here. You've got to trust me. I need your help. Together we—" He broke off as a sudden howl came from a machine at one side of the laboratory. An assistant stepped back from it, making a helpless gesture. "What's that?"

"I don't know. Interference of some kind. An unshielded power source."

The hybeam transmitter! His hand reached for his chest, muscles knotting as he fought the restraints. He urgently told the woman, "My chest. In the region of the heart. Feel for a nodule. Press it. Quickly, you fool! Press it!"

The howling died as she obeyed.

"My lady!" A guard, the twin of the one who still watched impassively from his station, came toward the couch. "Some trouble on the radionic detector. It was impossible to determine the level on the latest tissue samples."

"So?"

"They are ruined. Others must be provided. Will you please check on the functioning of the machine?"

"Send for Shign Baluka," she said coldly. "I am not an electronics engineer. Now please allow me to continue with my tests."

"You have influence," said Kennedy as the man backed away. "I wonder you haven't already used it."

"To escape?" She shrugged, her hands busy as she talked, her voice low. "That's impossible. There are passages leading upward but all are thick with guards. And don't make the mistake of thinking that I would be obeyed if I tried to give orders outside my laboratory. I am given the appearance of respect by the guards only because I am needed by Kaifeng. What is that device buried in your chest? A beacon?"

"Yes."

"I see." She glanced at the machine, the watchful guard. "So you were telling me the truth. You wanted to be taken so that you could be followed, is that it?" She didn't wait for an answer. "A good plan, but it couldn't work. The entire area here is screened. You saw what happened when the radionic tester was switched on. I was working with similar machines beyond the acceleration field when you arrived and I heard nothing. Not even seconds before I came to examine you. If anyone is listening for your signal they wouldn't hear it."

She didn't realize the full extent of the complication. If he had been transshipped to Kaifeng's vessel which could also have been screened—he remembered the lambent blue glow he'd seen before—then the *Mordain* might have lost him.

He said, "Is there a hybeam radio transmitter here? A communications shack?"

"I don't know."

"Think, woman!" His tone was harshly impatient. "There has to be one. Where would it be?"

"I don't know." She shook her head at his expression. "I woke up in a room just like you did. There was a girl, and I was taken to Kaifeng. He told me what I had to do—and he showed me that it was impossible to refuse. Since then I have been confined to the laboratory. Years of endless labor—it has to be years, my mirror tells me that. My mirror and my eyes. I remember Lars Horsen as he used to be. What he is now I shall become."

... Old, withered, senile, dying to serve a relentless

master, slave of a warped genius with a consuming ambition. Kennedy moved restlessly on the couch. Unless the *Mordain* was close he alone stood between Kaifeng and whatever plan he had in mind.

A hood was lowered over his face and he stared at winking darkness as instruments touched his body with minor stabs of pain.

"Don't be alarmed," whispered the woman. "I am merely taking a series of samples for more intensive examination. What do you hope to do?"

"Kill Kaifeng."

"You think it possible to do that?" Her voice was bleak, defeated. "He is always guarded. You might think him alone, but he never is. One of those who came before you tried it. What happened to him was something I would rather not remember. Kaifeng cannot be defeated."

She had said Kaifeng, not the master. At least she retained enough independence not to call him that. It gave Kennedy a hope, at least, that she might be an ally if he could persuade her to cooperate. And she was wrong about Keifeng. Any man could be killed. If he himself had to die while doing it, well, that was the luck of the game.

"Unstrap me," he said as the hood was lifted. He could not afford to wait for the others. If a chance presented itself he had to be ready to take it.

He threw his legs over the edge of the couch as the restraints fell away, stretching, apparently just looking around casually. One guard was standing beside the door through which they had entered, another by the portal Lars Horsen had used, two more among the assistants; none seeming to be taking a special interest. There were a handful of workers, a man heading toward the radionic detector, Laura Previn herself.

The man must have entered before the hood was lifted from Kennedy's face. Like Lars Horsen he was old, muttering to himself as he moved slowly over the floor. Shign Baluka was another victim of the enigmatic blue field.

He could be ignored, and so could the woman. The attendants would most likely leave any violent action to the guards. The one who had accompanied him from the cell would be the most alert, so Kennedy mentally selected the one standing beside the strange door. Once down, the device at his belt could be used against the others. Kennedy knew that he could move fast enough and withstand the pain long enough for him to get it.

He stretched again, turning, his hand falling to the machine at the side of the couch, the shining instrument he had seen there. It was a diagnostic tool of some kind, but it had mass and could be thrown to distract.

The lights pulsed, the shimmering blue radiance on the far wall flickered, then died, revealing a seamless surface of polished metal broken only by the outline of a single door.

"Kaifeng!" Laura Previn sucked in her breath. "He is coming. He—"

Kennedy moved. He threw himself from the side of the couch, the instrument glinting as he lifted his hand; he spun the glittering wheel toward the guard, aimed directly at his eyes. Instinctively the man lifted his hands to protect his face and then Kennedy was on him, one fist slamming into the stomach, the stiffened edge of the other chopping at the side of the man's neck.

Kennedy caught the lifeless body as it fell and turned it to face away from him. He rammed his thumb hard against the button at the top of the box-like buckle.

A guard screamed and doubled as he ran forward, blood reddening his mouth and chin from his bitten tongue. Two attendants joined him on the floor, a third backing desperately to avoid the muscle-cramping projection. Laura Previn watched, her mouth open, her eyes wide, one hand lifted to her throat.

Kennedy tugged at the belt, snarled as it held fast, then backed, reaching behind him toward the door the dead man had flanked.

He touched metal, found a knob, turned it and pushed, feeling a chill gush of air strike his back and shoulders. Dropping the dead man, he sprang backward into the opening and slammed the door. As he turned he saw a narrow passage flanked with doors, all closed. A cross passage lay at the end of the corridor and, as he reached it, a man stepped from the left—a guard who held a Dione.

Kennedy snatched at the guard's wrist with his right hand, sending the stiffened fingers of his left hand like a blunted spear into the spot beneath the man's ear. Snatching free the weapon as the guard fell, dead before he hit the floor, Kennedy jumped over the body and ran down the passage. He halted at the sound of a hatefully remembered voice.

"Halt! Move and you die!"

The threat was impossible to ignore. The passage was too long and too narrow; a blast from a Dione would catch him in the back, burning a hole through flesh and bone and internal organs, impaling him like an insect on a shaft of searing energy.

But if he could turn, fire a fraction before the other . . .

"Do not even consider it," purred the cold voice. "You are a man of logic, Captain Kennedy. Surely you do not imagine that I would expose myself to the suicidal act you contemplate. The weapon you hold is unloaded, merely a device to distract you. Try it if you wish."

Kennedy dropped, turning, pressing the trigger as he swerved. The gun gave a dry click. He rose, throwing it aside. A man had died to maintain the pretense, but men were cheap here.

He said flatly, "You have a strange sense of humor, Dr. Wei Kaifeng."

CHAPTER NINE

He was as Kennedy remembered, tall, richly dressed, the gemmed insignia of the double helix glowing like twin serpents on his breast. He was not alone. Tsing, his aide, stood next to him, and three armed guards stood in front.

Two others stood at the rear, Vivien Dreux between them.

"Cap," she said. "I'm sorry. I couldn't help it. I had to tell him. I—" She broke off, blinking, her eyes bright with unshed tears.

"A most charming person," said Kaifeng. "You must not blame her for divulging your identity. In fact, she told me nothing I did not already know. But you assumed she had been left behind on Weingold, of course. Or perhaps you didn't care. In many ways, Captain, you are a most ruthless man, as I have cause to know."

Kennedy made no comment.

"And naturally the girl is expendable. As you are yourself, Captain. How else to explain your presence here?" Kaifeng shrugged. "But enough. This is not the place to welcome an old adversary. There should be wine and soft music and something for you to learn. As the girl had learned, to her cost. We can dispense with her for the present, I think. Tsing, attend to it. And now, Captain, if you will be so good as to follow me, there is much we have to discuss."

"Such as, Doctor?"

"Many things. And you learn. You will learn more, but at least you accord me my title."

"Because you have earned it. The use to which you put your knowledge is another matter."

"And surely because to irritate an enemy without purpose is irrational behavior?" Kaifeng gestured with one slender hand. "After you, Captain."

The room fitted the man: luxurious, a little barbaric, softness coating an adamantine hardness. Watching as Keifeng took his chair, Kennedy wondered how many others had stood before it as he did now. He wondered what had been done to them to make them talk and cooperate. Soon, perhaps he would know.

"Vivien Dreux," said Keifeng musingly. "A young and lovely woman. Some men would have hesitated at placing her in a position of such danger but, as I have said, Captain, you are not an ordinary man. Some wine?"

"Thank you, no."

"You are cautious, but to no purpose. The wine is harmless and we should, at least, drink to the fact that we have something in common. You, like myself, have been to Sheol. You, like myself, have won the gamble with the Kriad. That, if nothing else, forms a bond. Tsing! Wine for our guest."

The man had softly entered the room. Now he came forward with a brimming glass. Kennedy pushed it aside.

"It is time, I think," said Kaifeng softly, "for you to learn a lesson. The next time I offer you a drink, Captain, you will not refuse."

He leaned forward a little, his face suffused with anticipation, the slender fingers of his hands resting on the arms of his throne-like chair.

"Now!"

Kennedy fell, engulfed in pain.

Different from the electronic whip, this was a tearing, sickening, cumulative agony which wrenched at the very fabric of his mind. For a moment he almost yielded to it, then stubbornly he began to fight back using the Clume Discipline and the Ghengarch System of Disorientation, one to achieve mastery of his body, the other to obtain a remote detachment. Pain is a nervous response to appropriate stimuli which training can lessen, even negate, and Kennedy had been well trained. The agony remained but he blocked it, diminished it to bearable proportions, thrust it in to a far corner of his mind as he relived the previous few moments.

Kaifeng leaned forward, his hands on the arms of his chair. Had one of the fingers depressed a stud?

"You will drink," whispered Kaifeng. "I command you to drink and what I command you will do. Refuse and again you will beg for release from pain."

"No."

The flood of agony came again, but this time there was no doubt. The finger had tensed, which meant there had to be a control, a trigger for some invisible force. Whether it worked on the body or the nerves like the electronic whip didn't matter; what did was the fact that he could absorb and handle the pain.

"Incredible!" Kaifeng narrowed his eyes as he stared at the kneeling figure. "A man in a billion, Tsing. One who refuses to be broken. Given time it could be done, but doing it would ruin his mind and his body—a waste I wish to avoid. There could be another way."

His vanity betrayed him. A man with more sense or less pride would have killed out of hand, but Kaifeng was too devious to take the simple way. Kennedy rose to his feet as the pain died, recognizing his chance, the other's basic need.

"To be at the summit of a mountain, Doctor, is to be in a lonely place."

"As you know, Captain."

"As I have heard. There is no one to understand you, none in whom to confide. Success is diminished by being unshared, failure—"

"I do not fail!"

"Perhaps not, but what of those you have to entrust with your plans! Do they never fail?"

They both recalled the ship which should have been destroyed, the trail left which should have been covered. Other things.

"It was once said by a military genius," said Kennedy quietly, "that given three men he could trust he would conquer the world. Have you three such men, Doctor? Have you one?"

Kaifeng said, "Follow me."

The passages they entered led to compartments filled with animal stinks, cages of things that crept and fluttered.

"Birds," said the doctor. "Manufactured to strict requirements by my genetic staff. They can eat anything, survive in all temperatures, are pleasant to look at and make soothing noises—and their droppings contain a virulent bacteria which will attack and kill all life other than their own. The bacteria can, of course, be adapted to any world."

Kennedy asked, "Their rate of propagation?"

"High. They will fill the skies before the danger is even realized."

Keifeng passed on to a stunted thing cowering behind a heap of stones. "A rodent with teeth capable of gnawing through steel and concrete. Power lines, communication cables, transport systems, none would be safe. You see, Captain, I learned much from the Kriad."

"Biological warfare isn't new, Doctor. You may have refined it, but life can always be defeated by other forms of life."

"Perhaps, but consider, Captain, the power such an ability gives to a world. A few eggs deposited in a secluded place and the economy would be crippled for a decade."

"Crippled or spurred? History tells us that both technology and economic growth are stimulated by internal conflict." Kennedy shrugged. "But then I am talking of Earth."

"Earth," whispered Kaifeng. "And the men of Earth. Those who destroyed my base on Papan, who almost destroyed my ship. Do you think I have forgotten what you did?"

"Tried to do, Doctor, and obviously failed to do. You were the target, not your ship."

For a moment Kennedy thought he had gone too far, that Kaifeng would turn and order Tsing to kill him where he stood; then Kaifeng gave a curious gesture, as if dismissing the past or anticipating a pleasurable future. He was a man eager to talk, to spin his fabric of dreams, to terrify possibly, certainly to gloat.

"A man can respect a worthy adversary, Captain, and you have shown yourself to be that. But what has it gained you? What can Terran Control with all its wealth and power give you? You will always have superiors. You will never be allowed to form your own destiny. At each turn your fate will be decided by others." He emphasized the word a little, repeating it. "Fate, Captain, an irony when you think about it. On Sheol you gambled and yet what did you win? The life of a friend—and where is that friend now? I also gambled and received the potential mastery of the universe. I am willing to gamble again. Join me. Work with me. Share in what is to come."

Kennedy said slowly, "I came to find five missing scientists. I didn't even know you were still alive."

"And now that you do?"

He had a duty to perform, a threat to be negated, Kaifeng himself to be executed for past crimes and for future safety, but Kennedy knew better than to say it. Deviousness had to be met and dealt with in the same coin. Lies had to be turned against the liar; promises must apparently be taken seriously and considered as viable propositions. It was the only way he could hope to survive.

"I didn't expect such an offer. I must admit that I'm interested."

"I shall, of course, require proof of your sincerity, Captain—information. But that can come later. For now, all I require of you is proof of your willingness to obey."

"Proof," said Kennedy. "Doesn't that work both ways?"

"What do you mean?"

"You ask me to join you, but join what? Some underground laboratory where you manufacture adapted forms of life? I could see as much in the Bovosk Institute on

Earth. Some guards who act like zombies? Some big talk and dreams? If I join you I throw away my life, Doctor, the life I have known. Just what are you offering in exchange?"

"An empire!" Kaifeng drew in his breath, seeming to expand, to grow even taller, a man entranced. "Worlds for your playthings, women, luxuries, men to command. More wealth and power than you have ever imagined—all will be yours if you obey me. You have an imagination, Captain, use it! Earth itself could be your footstool."

Kaifeng's bribe rested on the lowest of human emotions, greed, and Kennedy said dryly. "A man can only eat so much, Doctor. He can only be in one place at a time. And excess brings satiation. What you offer is boredom."

"You are right, Captain, and you are a shrewd man to have realized it, but before the spirit can soar the flesh must be satisfied. And think of what the offer implies. Men to do your bidding, factories to build your constructions, planets devoted to the solving of a single problem. How often have you been hampered by the need of money or men? Join me and your word will be law. The most closely guarded secrets will yield their innermost mysteries. Power, my friend. Real power. The ability to control the destiny of worlds."

The prospect was entrancing and Kennedy pondered it, knowing that it was expected of him. Entire scientific institutions could work toward a single objective. The enigma of the Zheltyana would finally be solved—the secrets of the Ancient Race, their beginning and end, their incredible knowledge all clear at last. Poverty would be eradicated, peace ensured, the Golden Age become a concrete reality.

Kennedy drew in his breath like a man obviously overwhelmed as old loyalties dissolved beneath the impact of the glittering prospect.

"But how can this be done, Doctor? How can you, one man, achieve so much?"

Kaifeng smiled, a quirk of the lips more of satisfaction than humor, a grimace which held contempt.

"Come, " he said. "You shall see."

They entered passages through native stone, compartments filled with humming machines, storerooms, dormitories, workshops, reservoirs of water, depositories of food, gigantic accumulations of power—a fortress holding a laboratory which held in turn the fruits of a warped genius.

The display was born of Kaifeng's need to boast, to be acclaimed, to be recognized for what he was. He was proud of the seed which would grow and expand to engulf entire planets, systems, the galaxy itself . . . Kaifeng's domain.

It was not hard for Kennedy to appear impressed, and it was easy for him to pretend that he was eager to become part of the colossal plan. He knew they made twin covers for his crystalized resolve that all this, no matter what the cost, must be destroyed.

"And here is where we shall begin." Kaifeng gestured toward a line of transparent caskets ranked like coffins in an echoing chamber. Blue fire embraced them and, at the side of each, pumps softly whined as they fed in nutrients. "Cells taken from those who won at the games, prime specimens of the human frame. They were placed in sterile eggs and stimulated to grow in artificial wombs. Clone-men, each exactly like the other, all the best of their type."

Kennedy stepped toward the caskets, feeling a slight tingle from the blue field, the time-accelerator which worked its peculiar magic. Within the caskets lay men, seeming to grow even as he watched, muscle shaping itself around bone, tissue filling hollows, sinew thickening beneath the skin.

"Empty vessels as yet," murmured Kaifeng. "When fully grown they will be taken from the caskets and their brains filled with a selected pattern of knowledge. Certain attributes will be emphasized: the desire to kill, the need to obey, the necessity of combat. They will be an army fashioned to any requirement. Better than mercenaries, more adaptable than volunteers, quickly grown and quickly trained, they would have appeal to many."

. . . To the Chambodians at least, Kennedy reflected, who were always hungry to expand their Complex. To the Haddrach of Holme, always short of warriors. To a dozen races restrained from war only by their limited resources. To them Kaifeng would sell his techniques, supplying the means to fashion an overhwleming force. Once used, these cloned humans would send an engulfing wave of hatred toward Earth. And each of them would carry, implanted in the deepest recesses of his brain, the overriding command that his first obedience was to Kaifeng. A hidden danger would be poised at the backs of their employers—an army waiting only the word to strike, to place their first master on the galactic throne.

"You see, my friend, I shall not be alone." Kaifeng's gesture was casual. "This is only the beginning. Here and on a hundred worlds I will have an endless supply of dedicated warriors. The best the human race can provide."

Kennedy turned, seeing a guarded door further down the chamber. He casually moved toward it.

"Hold!" Kaifeng's voice was the thinly cutting lash of a whip. "You have seen enough. Give me your answer. Will you join me?"

"Have I any choice?"

"None. You agree or you die, but dying you will serve me anyway. Your body duplicated a million times, clones from your flesh obeying me to the end. You see, Captain, I think highly of you. So highly that I ask for little proof of your sincerity. But that proof I must have."

"Proof?"

"The girl," said Kaifeng blandly. "The one who was taken with you. Vivien Dreux. You will kill her."

CHAPTER TEN

Against the cold light of distant stars the *Mordain* was an insignificant fleck of glimmering metal, drifting without power, the ports masked, apparently lifeless. Only the suited figure working with desperate intensity on the hull showed that it was not just another scrap of interstellar debris.

Tiny glows accompanied it, the trace of Saratov's las-torch. He was hurriedly welding slender rods of metal into a complex lattice. He moved with deft skill, ignoring the sweat running down his face, stinging his eyes and a raw place on the side of his neck, a patch caused by a too hastily adjusted helmet.

"Penza?" Chemile's voice was anxious. "You'd better come in now."

"Not yet, Veem."

"Your air must be getting low."

Saratov grunted, glancing at the dial, noting that it registered empty. But the lattice was almost finished, and to enter the ship to replace his tank would take valuable time.

"Tell Jarl to start testing. I'll be in as soon as I've finished."

"You won't help Cap by dying, Penza."

"And we won't help him wasting time in a lot of gab. If you want to help, bring me out a fresh tank. Jarl?"

"Ready, Penza."

"How's it look?"

Luden checked instruments and watched the kick of

needles in the laboratory. The monitor bench was filled with a jumble of apparatus, breadboard circuitry hastily improvised but efficient despite its appearance.

"So far things are going as expected, Penza," he said in his precise tones. "I can't be sure, of course, until the scanner is complete. How much longer will it take?"

"A few more minutes." A grunt and then, "Damn it, Jarl, I'm getting sloppy. Have Veem bring me out more air."

"I'm here, you big ox." Chemile's voice was tense over the speakers. "Now hold still while I make the switch. Anything more I can do?"

"Make some coffee. I'll need it when this is done."

The percolator was bubbling when Saratov entered the ship, his face red, his eyes sore as he doffed the suit. Gripping the cup Chemile offered him in one big hand he thrust his way into the laboratory.

"Well, Jarl?"

"I'm not sure yet, Penza." Luden adjusted a vernier, frowned at the lack of response. "Veem, take the controls and turn the *Mordain* in a complete circle. Go slowly and stand ready to halt if I give the word."

"Do you think it's going to work, Jarl?"

"I don't know, Veem," confessed Luden. "We are working on the basis of pure theory. It should logically be possible to amplify the range of the Larvic-Shaw; also, by installing filters to block out spatial noise, we should be able to isolate nodes of gravitational disturbance. The trouble is that, in order to gain range and eliminate as much interference as possible, we have to use a narrow scan, a tight cone which can only cover a limited area of space. With luck we can use a wide angle and cut down to acute scan once a node has been spotted, but a lot depends on just where we look."

Too much, as they all knew. Space was vast and even a world was small in comparison, a minute fleck easily lost among the scattered suns. And they were not looking for a world but a ship—the vessel which had vanished into space at incredible speed.

"It had to land somewhere," said Luden. "We have

already determined that Kaifeng must be operating from a base and it is logical to assume that it would be within easy range of a common point." He gestured to the mass of reports which littered the table, the stellar charts laced with spider-like lines, the graphs from the computers on Earth and within the *Mordain*. "We know the *Shardorn* was attacked midway between Krone and Weingold. Cap was transshipped at about the same point. Weyburn has combed all agent reports for details of unusual purchases of electronic or biochemical materials. We have five planets where such purchases were made. Seven others on which they could have been transshipped, twenty-six more which could have been used as assembly points. They all have a common center. Unfortunately, it encompasses rather a large area."

That was an understatement. The area was a sphere more than a parsec in diameter, a volume of space containing over thirty cubic light-years. In such an area even the solar system would be minute.

"However," continued Luden as if he were lecturing, a sure sign of his inward strain, "we can reduce the effective search-area by half. With elimination of predicted spatial distortions we can reduce that even more. Unfortunately, there are no suns within the area, which means that Kaifeng's base must be either an artificial construction or a rogue planetoid. I tend to think it must be the latter. He would need the raw materials and the space it would provide, for one thing. Something of the nature of Ceres, perhaps. Such a planetoid, from Kaifeng's point of view, would be ideal."

"Ceres," said Saratov, "has a diameter of less than five hundred miles. Well, it's bigger than a ship."

"I said something of the nature of Ceres," corrected Luden. "It need not have the actual dimensions. Of course, the larger it is the more chance we shall have of spotting it. Veem!"

Chemile was already at the controls. Luden concentrated on his instruments and Saratov checked the writhing lines on the Larvic-Shaw monitor against the information gathered by the external lattice. Chemile sent the

Mordain in a slowly expanding spherical spiral, a complex pattern which would search every inch of surrounding space.

Then, suddenly, Saratov shouted, "I've got something, Jarl!"

"Right, Penza, I've got it now too. It looks like we may have been correct."

A long job and one which couldn't be hurried. As the hours dragged past they fell into a routine, one resting while the others kept watch, all uneasily conscious of the passage of time.

"This could take months," rumbled Saratov. He had brewed coffee and stood with the cup in his hand glaring at the instruments. "Is there nothing we could do to speed things up, Jarl?"

"No, Penza." Luden was due to rest, but was reluctant to leave his instruments. "Once we break the search-pattern we will be operating on a basis of random selection—luck. And I shouldn't have to remind you that luck comes in two kinds."

"Good and bad," admitted the giant. "As yet we've had nothing but bad." He lifted the cup to his lips then froze the action. "Jarl! The detectors!"

Something had registered, the Larvic-Shaw screen a mass of cojoining lines. Slipping into his seat Luden donned earphones and made a careful adjustment of a vernier. Outside the scanner moved a little as he concentrated on obtaining the highest noise-gain from the instruments.

"Jarl?"

"Something is heading this way, Penza. It could be a meteorite or some other scrap of debris, but I don't think so. Have you got it, Veem?"

"It's moving fast, Jarl." Chemile was anxious. "Should I try to match it?"

"No, Veem." Luden lifted the earphones. "I think it may be a ship; if so, we don't want to betray ourselves. Hold position and track with the scanner. Penza, take readings at two-second intervals alternate with mine. Mark! Now!"

They worked like machines, eyes darting to the screens, fingers deft on the graphed paper. The node of disturbance came relatively closer, passed, streaked away at an incredible velocity.

"Veem! Aim the scanner after it. Take an aligned position and follow at sub-light velocity."

"That's only a crawl, Jarl!"

"It will give us a flight path and enable us to escape detection." Luden turned to his figures and made a quick calculation. "Penza?"

"It was traveling fast, Jarl, but I think it was slowing. Allowing for the Doppler effect, it had to be."

"I agree." Luden pursed his thin lips as he compared the two sets of notations. "If we extend the flight line—so, then the vessel must have originated somewhere in the region of the Elkard Cluster. Continued, it would lead to—"

"Nowhere," finished Saratov. "It would follow a path to the rim of the galaxy and beyond. Which means that it must be heading for Kaifeng's base. It could even have been his ship."

"Or one identical to it, Penza. Certainly it had the same characteristics as the vessel which took Cap. If it is the same one, they must have taken Cap to the base and then moved on toward the Elkard Cluster, perhaps to pick up supplies from a waiting vessel. In any case we now have a flight path to follow."

"Then let's follow it." The giant was impatient. "God knows what that devil is doing to Cap, but we can guess it won't be pleasant." He looked at his big hands; they were clenched into fists. "I want to deal with Kaifeng personally if he has hurt Cap. This time there'll be no chance of him coming alive again. I'll tear him into shreds."

Luden shared the emotion, but as always he saw other probabilities.

"We don't know that he has yet recognized Cap, Penza. Unless they met face to face he would have no reason to suspect him. After all, he was only the winner of the games at Weingold. If Kaifeng remained on his ship he would have had little time to make an investigation. But I agree, we have no time to waste. Veem!"

"Ready to move, Jarl?"

"The object we observed was slowing, Veem. That means the base must be within a light-year from our present position. Take a course at right angles to the vessel, following an inward curve." Luden gave the co-ordinates. "Once we spot the base on the scanner we can drop velocity and drift in to land."

"Got it, Jarl. Here we go!"

The instruments danced, the stars on the screens flickered, then steadied again as they passed plus-C velocity. Crouched over the panel, Luden made adjustments and a series of notations, grunting with satisfaction as he found the relevant node.

"There it is, Penza. Without that ship passing close and giving us a line we could have searched for it for years. See?" He pointed to the writhing lines on the Larvic-Shaw. "Exactly the same configuration as a natural vortex . . . the typical pattern of a high-density, low-volume spatial distortion."

"If Cap is there, Jarl, why can't we pick up his transmission?"

"Three possible reasons, Penza: Cap isn't there, he isn't transmitting or, if he is transmitting, then the signal is blocked by a screen. I think the last is the most likely possibility. If the place wasn't screened we would have picked up radiated energy long before this. The mere fact that it is screened makes me practically certain that we have found what we were looking for. We will know for sure once we land."

And once they had landed they could rescue Cap, thought Luden bleakly . . . rescue him if it were humanly possible, avenge him if it were not, Cap and the woman with him. They must not forget the girl.

She stood in the cell looking very young and very lovely. She came forward as the door slammed shut, almost running, throwing herself into his arms.

"Cap! Thank God you're still alive! I was so afraid

for you and I knew it was all my fault. How can you ever forgive me?"

"There's nothing to forgive." Kennedy held her close, feeling the warmth of her body, the pressure, the demand for reassurance as she clung to him. The girl was very much afraid and more than a little ashamed. "You couldn't help it."

"I tried, but the pain . . ." She shuddered. "I've never felt such pain before. He said it was caused by a poison in my blood, that I would die if I didn't get the antidote at regular intervals. And he questioned me. I tried not to answer but—"

His hand lifted to stroke her hair. Its scent was that of summer flowers, of freshly cut wheat, of sun and golden pollen.

"It's over now," he said. "All over. And you haven't been poisoned; that was a lie. It was just some electronic gadgetry."

"You're sure?"

"I'm sure. He tried it out on me."

"And you took it?" She leaned back a little so she could stare into his eyes, her head uptilted, her hair a curtain over her shoulders. "You took it," she said. "But you would. As I said once before, a long time ago it seems now, you are a very special kind of man."

"As you are a woman."

"Your woman, Cap. I suppose every girl dreams of meeting a man like you. I guess I was lucky. I know that it can't last, but I'm grateful for what I've had. Maybe you should be angry at the way I took advantage, but I don't regret it. You warned me, but I wouldn't listen. Now I guess I'm just a burden."

"You're an agent of Terran Control," he said, his lips close to her ear. "Remember that."

"Does it matter what I was now?"

"It matters. We still have a job to do."

"Yes." She took a deep breath. "Keep talking, Cap. I like you to hold me like this even though you're probably only doing it so no one can overhear. Well, what happened? What did Kaifeng say?"

"He made me an offer. He wants me to join him."

"And you agreed," she said instantly. "You would have had to. It gives you a chance. Was there anything else?"

"One thing." Kennedy tightened his arms around the slim, lithe body. "He ordered me to kill you."

He felt her tense, her muscles bunching like springs under his hands, a creature shocked into sudden fear. Then she relaxed and when she spoke her voice was flatly calm, the words a statement of fact.

"Then you will have to do it, Cap. If you hope to beat Kaifeng you'll have to play the game his way until you get your chance. Did . . ." Her voice faltered a little. "Did he say how it should be done?"

"No."

"Or when?"

"No, but it will have to be soon." Kennedy lifted his hands and closed them around the slender throat. Men would be watching—he had to make it look convincing—but there was still time.

"Listen and remember what I say. My ship, the *Mordain,* has to be close. Killing you will gain me time."

"So you have to kill me," she said dully. "God, Cap, I understand. What's one life against the safety of Earth?"

Nothing, Cap thought, and he would kill her and anyone else if it was the only way to save the planet . . . kill her no matter how close they had been, no matter how much she loved him. And she did love him—as much as he loved Earth.

"Listen,"' he said again. "There is a woman, Laura Previn. They will take you to her. You must persuade her to help us. There are others—she knows who—but this is what she must do."

He spelled it out, his mouth close to her ear, his hands plain around her throat, his elbows lifting as he tightened his fingers.

"Now struggle, damn you! Struggle! I'm killing you, remember. Killing you!"

She put on a good show. Twice he allowed her to scream, once releasing her to watch, gloatingly, her wide eyes and shocked expression before gripping her again, twisting to avoid an upjerked knee, burying his face in her hair to save his eyes from her raking nails. Then he closed his hands, the fingers searching for the carotids, the sensitive nerves which would bring unconsciousness and paralysis, a simulated death to defy casual inspection.

And, as he had known they would, guards immediately came running to carry the limp body away.

"You please me, my friend." Kaifeng stood beyond the bars of the cell, his eyes filled with a gloating pleasure. "You please me very much. After all, Captain, what is one woman more or less? The companion of the moment, is it not so? A weakness of the masculine condition. And yet they have their uses, as you have seen—as objects of tests, if nothing else. There will be other tests. But enough for now. There are matters to which I must attend before we meet again. In the meantime sit and compose yourself. Think of what you have just done—and dwell on the utter futility of anyone ever hoping to delude Kaifeng!"

CHAPTER ELEVEN

The mirror did not lie. Laura Previn stared into it, one hand lifting to touch the thick streaks of gray in her hair, the pouched eyes, the creped skin of throat and cheeks. She had been a beautiful woman once; she remembered the captain of the *Shardorn,* his obvious admiration. And there had been others, long ago now, a lifetime ago it seemed. No, not seemed, was. They had remained young or as they had been while she had grown old.

Old!

The glass shattered as she struck it and she stared blankly at the blood on her hand, the dark bruises at the knuckles. Why couldn't the mirror have been Kaifeng?

She felt the anger rise again as she thought of him and the trick he had played, the life he had wasted—her life and others too, but hers above all.

She thought of the sunshine she had missed, the company of friends, their envy perhaps, certainly their honest praise. What work she might have done, what new discoveries she could have made—and all the little things which went to soften the impact of years so, that, at the end, she could have rested knowing she had done her best for the good of all.

Kaifeng!

The thought of him was a sickness, the hate a corrosive venom eating at her brain. Horsen was mad, babbling to himself in senile ramblings, due to be eliminated as soon as his master thought of a way to wring the last scrap of diseased pleasure from his death; until then he was allowed to exist in his miserable hell. Baluka was little better; he had retained an animal-like cunning. Cayus—she didn't like to think of what had happened to the biochemist, but would her end be any different?

Could her position be any worse than it was now?

She heard the sound of tittering and caught herself, horrified at the knowledge that the senile laughter had come from her own throat. Not that! Dear God, not that! At least let her die with dignity.

The passage outside her room was empty—what need of guards for those conditioned by pain? Baluka resided three doors down. Once the arrangement had been convenient when they found brief happiness in mutual embraces, but that had been long ago. The relationship could still have its uses, however, for some memories never faded and he had loved her in his fashion.

He whined as she opened the door, lying as usual in darkness, curled up on the bed in a fetal position. The light hurt his eyes and he covered them a hand blotched with ugly spots of brown.

"Shign!" His shoulder trembled beneath her hand. "Shign, it's Laura. Laura, your friend."

"Leave me alone!"

Sighing, she lifted the hypogun loaded with its carefully blended charge of drugs. Chemicals to shock the mind back to an awareness of reality, the compounds gave strength at the expense of longevity. The magic had been created in her laboratories for just such a need. He flinched as air blasted the drugs into his blood, but when he turned his eyes were clear.

"Laura, my dear! This is a pleasure."

"Get up, Shign. You have work to do."

"Work?"

"Here." She handed him a hypogun, a twin of the one she had used but loaded with the time-stasis drug she had made under Kaifeng's direction: his knowledge, her labor, a fair exchange. "You will go down into the electronics room and kill the screen. You understand? You will kill the screen."

"But why? For what purpose?"

The girl hadn't told her, she had only insisted that it be done.

"You will do it." The drugs had contained a hypnotic medium and repetition emphasized the command. "You will kill the screen. If anyone tries to stop you use the hypogun. You will kill the screen."

"I don't understand." His lips trembled as his eyes turned from her, an animal trapped and seeking escape. Again she blasted drugs into his bloodstream. The dose was probably too heavy, but what use would he make of the remainder of his life?

And how was it possible now, Laura asked herself, to remember him as the lover he had once been?

"Do it, Shign. Kill the screen. You have a right to check the installation. If anyone tries to prevent you then use the hypogun. You are to kill the screen." And then, in a flash of inspiration, she added, "Kaifeng orders it. The master must be obeyed."

"Yes," he muttered. "Yes, the master must always be obeyed."

"Then do it. Now!"

She stepped back as he rose, watching as he left the room and headed down the passage toward the lower regions. Perhaps he would fail. Perhaps his brain would yield too soon, or his strength, but that was beyond her ability to control. Like a thing of clockwork, he had been wound and set on his way. She could do no more; she had already risked too much as it was, but others had risked more and she had a duty toward them.

The girl had been willing to die—had in fact almost died—but she had recovered just in time to whisper her instructions. The girl was strong in more ways than one, Laura Previn reflected, just as Kennedy was a man who was far from ordinary.

He looked up from where he sat in his barred cell, not speaking, only his eyes moving toward her, past her, searching, she guessed, for guards.

"We are alone." She came close to the bars, conscious of his personality, the masculinity which could not be disguised. "There are no guards in this passage. There will be some farther down toward the audience chamber, but not many. They are busy."

"At what?"

"A demonstration." She caught herself on the verge of tittering. "Kaifeng is showing off his wares. Those who would buy are watching. Soon . . ." She broke off, unwilling to say more.

"Soon?"

"Never mind. Don't you want to know about the girl?"

"She is alive. The fact that you are here proves that."

"Alive and well, though you almost pressed too hard. If it hadn't been for the stimulation of the electronic probe she might have succumbed. Her ovaries," she explained. "The eggs from her body to contain new life—even if she had really died they would have been viable. And there were other things Kaifeng wished to obtain. You knew he would, of course."

The heart of the gamble he had won. But they had both won. Kennedy said, "Where is she now?"

"In a safe place."

"Where?"

"In the laboratory, of course. She was supposed to be dead. I placed her in a small chamber next to the one containing the vats of the clone-men. For a while she is safe."

"And the screen?"

"It will be attended to if Shign does as I asked. He left to do it. I cannot guarantee that he will succeed."

"I didn't ask for guarantees," said Kennedy. "But thank you for what you have done."

"There is one thing I cannot do. I have no means of opening your cell."

"Have you anything of metal about you?"

"No." She had left the hypogun back in Shign's room. She wore no rings and her dress was held with plastic fasteners. "Tell me, is it true what the girl said about the pain? That it was caused by an adaptation of the electronic whip and not by a poison induced into my metabolism?"

"It's true."

"All this time," she whispered. "Years and years during which I've lived in constant fear. Even escape seemed out of the question—what use to escape when agony rides with you? And it was all a cruel deception. A sadistic whim of a deranged beast. Years! A lifetime!"

... Years for her, days for others, that mystery was still only half explained.

"You saw the blue glow," she said bleakly when he asked. "It is the visible effect of the time-acceleration field. Time enfolded in it moves ten times faster than it does outside. Ten times, but that was too slow for Kaifeng. He used the cascade principle—need I say more?"

That meant placing a field within a field within a field. Ten times magnification for the first, a hundred for the second, a thousand for the third. For her, years had passed in a single day.

"You came too late," she said bleakly. "But you could not know that, and you came. That I shall remember. At times courage needs a spur and you have given it to me. You and the girl. Now I have found the strength to do more than I intended. At least I shall try. When I die I shall not die alone."

Her hand reached out in mute appeal and Kennedy rose, taking it, applying gentle pressure to the thin fingers. Her face was pathetic framed in the bars, a ghost of its former self.

"Laura Previn, you are a brave woman."

"No. Not that. I have waited too long."

"Brave," he repeated emphatically. "Courage is the ability to do what has to be done when it needs to be done. You have it. You have always had it."

"Thank you." For a moment her face glowed and she was almost young again. "Goodbye, Cap. I'm sorry that I can't help you more, but you too have courage. Goodbye."

And then she was gone to find the others who had grown old at her side, to help her in what he had asked, what she had secretly intended—a secret best left to herself alone.

Kennedy stooped and examined the bars. They were thick, closely set, buried in the stone at roof and floor. A crossbar held them in the center, leaving four feet of inflexible metal above and below. The door fitted close, the hinges external, the lock a solid box without an inner opening. The edges of the door were tight to the jamb, making it impossible to get at the wards or latch.

He returned to the cot, a thin tubular frame with a thick plastic cover held by a series of loops. The legs lifted the frame a foot from the floor. Kneeling, he gripped one, muscles bunching in his back and shoulders as he worked the metal backward and forward, baring his teeth in satisfaction as the weakened metal gave and left the thin tube in his hand. As a weapon it left much to be desired, being too light and too thin, but he intended it and another he obtained for a different purpose.

Back at the bars he thrust his fingers into the thick mass of his hair, found what he wanted and jerked. The strand came free from where it had been imbedded in his scalp, an apparent hair, thicker than the rest, but of the same color. He passed it around the foot of a bar, wrapped each end around a leg of the bed and, holding one leg in each hand, pulled steadily at the thin strand.

The protective film fell from the thin wire it had masked, leaving a monofilament which was literally all edge, incredibly tough and harder than any diamond. It sliced through the crystalline interior bonds of the metal, Kennedy moving it from side to side as he pulled to prevent the cut surfaces adhering in a Johanssen weld. As it came free he repeated the process at the upper end of the bar, catching it as it fell; then he sliced through the one next to it to make an opening wide enough for his body.

Once in the passage he pressed the nodule activating the transmitter in his chest and, a heavy bar in each hand, stepped toward the end of the corridor.

Kaifeng's boasting had provided essential data; Kennedy had made a mental map of the installation as he was shown around, filling in details by obvious association. The laboratories would lie ahead, the girl would be beyond them. Once he had reached her he could make his way upward to where a passage led to an air lock connecting with the surface.

There would be suits there. If they could get them, break out into the surface, there would be a chance the *Mordain* could pick them up.

If the *Mordain* was in the vicinity. If the lock held usable suits. If he could manage to clear a path before Kaifeng turned the full garrison of the base against him.

A guard stood at the entrance to the laboratory. He gaped then died, a thrown bar slamming through his eye into the brain beneath. Kennedy paused only long enough to exchange the thin robe he wore for the dead man's uniform before he entered the chamber, a bar in his right hand, the thumb of his left resting on the button of the electronic whip at his belt. He pressed it as a guard turned toward him, the man's screams ending with the dull impact of the bar against his skull. Another, stepping from behind a machine, ran forward with manic desperation, the fields meeting, tearing at muscle and sinew, creating a red tide of mutual agony which ended as Kennedy used the bar again.

Panting, he looked around. The laboratory was deserted, the attendants busy at other tasks, only the two guards left as a routine force. The far wall glowed with a shimmer of blue radiance. Beyond it would lie the vats of the clone-men. Vivien had to be close.

He found her in the smallest of three chambers. She lay supine on a narrow cot, dressed in a thin white robe, her chest barely moving. Her eyes were closed and she seemed to be asleep or drugged.

"Up!" His hand slapped her cheek; there was no time to be gentle. "Wake up, Vivien!"

"What—" Her eyes opened, widening as they saw his face. "Cap! How did you get here?"

"Can you move? Are you drugged?"

"No, I don't think so." She threw her legs over the edge of the cot and stood upright, swaying a little.

"Laura gave me something and it made me feel all detached. I was dozing, daydreaming . . ." She shook her head, irritated at her weakness. "I'll be all right in a moment."

"Are you sure?" A faucet stood over a bowl in the corner. Kennedy ran water and dashed it into her face. "Better now? Good. We've got to get moving."

"Where?"

"Up and out if we can make it. Now stay close and duck if you have to. Let's go!"

A shout echoed through the laboratory as they left the chamber, guards spilling through the door by which Kennedy had entered. He gave them one glance and then ran to the far wall with its shimmer of blue. The door he had spotted opened and he slammed it behind them.

"Can't you lock it, Cap?"

"No need. We're moving ten times as fast as they are now. We're in a time-acceleration field. Just be sure you don't run into anything."

The place was as he remembered, the ranked coffin-like caskets, the chill air, the cold light. But now the pumps were silent, the caskets empty, their contents gone, he guessed, for the demonstration Laura Previn had mentioned. He paused for a moment, considering. That door ahead led to the upper chamber where he had been shown the mutated animals, the genetically fabricated birds. That other must lead away from the part of the installation he had inspected, probably down toward the lower levels. He headed toward the third, the door which had been guarded—which was guarded still—but on the other side.

One guard died beneath the smashing impact of the bar, another screamed, hands lifted to protect his eyes from Vivien's nails, but he followed his companion to the floor in broken ruin.

From a doorway down a narrow passage a man looked at the carnage.

He was small, stooped, his face seamed and lined, his eyes like sores in the strained pallor of his face.

Ghen Valdemar, cytologist, one of the five Kennedy had come to find.

"You mustn't come in here," he babbled. "You mustn't hurt her."

"Her?"

"She's special. I used all my art and skill—even Laura admitted that I'd done a wonderful job. That's why she didn't insist that I help her. She knew I had to stay here. Horsen agreed and so did Baluka, I think. Or was it Cayus? No, it couldn't have been Marl, he's dead."

Kennedy said gently, "What are they going to do? Horsen and the others? Baluka was to have killed the screen."

"I know. He's done that. Now he and Horsen are going to destroy the base. The power—they are going to do something with the atomic piles. I don't know what but they are going to do it. And they mustn't, not really, she is too perfect to waste."

Kennedy stepped past him into the chamber.

It was small, richly decorated, a shrine to scientific achievement. In the center rested an open casket and, lying in it, dressed in cloth of gold, the gemmed insignia of the double helix glinting on her breast, was the epitome of female grace.

She was tall and long-boned, with hips and thighs merging into a narrow waist that spread to rounded shoulders and slender arms. The breasts were high, full and proud, the neck a poem of loveliness, but it was the face which caught Cap's eyes.

The face was framed in a wealth of shimmering hair as black as the uttermost regions of space itself, the somber hue accentuating the delicate skin drawn taut over prominent bones. The cheeks were concave, hollows of mathematical precision accentuating the high cheekbones, the elfin line of the jaw. The mouth was full, the lower lip pouting a little to show perfect teeth as white as freshly driven snow. The forehead was high, fine bone and finer hair arching the brows. The eyes, open, were slanted elongations, abnormally wide, the irises lambent pools of violet.

But they were empty eyes, as blank as the windows of a deserted house, as empty as the brain behind them was. The newly grown brain had yet to be filled with knowledge and experience.

"Cap!" Vivien's voice was sharp. "Cap!"

He turned. The girl was standing at the door, her eyes bright with something, jealousy perhaps? Valdemar, muttering, took up his place beside the casket, an artist defending his creation.

"He did something," she said. "Pressed an alarm, I think. Cap, we've got to get out of here!"

CHAPTER TWELVE

Ges Zalk was a tall man with a sharp face and a pronounced widow's peak of hair. His nose was like a beak and his eyes were slotted like those of a bird. His hands, long-fingered, sharp-nailed, resembled claws. He was a Chambodian; everything about him betrayed his avian ancestry.

"Doctor, it is a pleasure to meet you."

Kaifeng ignored the outstretched hand. The gesture was foreign to Chambodians, though common to Terrestrials. The touch of empty palms signified peaceful intentions, a desire for friendship. Here friendship had no place—the man had come on business.

"Would you care for wine?"

"Thank you, no."

"Something else?"

Ges Zalk made no answer, no longer troubling to hide his disdain. He had no time for theatricals and had only grudgingly consented to the arrangements made by the agent on Elmay: the disguise, the ship which had taken him to the planet of the Elkard Cluster, another which had carried him into space, there to be transshipped and finally brought here to this unknown destination.

He had followed the orders because he'd had no choice. He could ignore them only at the cost of his career and personal loss of regard—a thing intolerable to any high-caste member of his race.

"You are disturbed, Colonel." Kaifeng made a small gesture. "Yes, I know who you are. I have my own means of checking just as you have yours. Let me make one thing plain. You are here because of my invitation. You have come to observe and to report back to your superiors. They are interested in what I have to offer even if you are not. But Colonel, I advise you to be very interested."

A threat? Ges Zalk stiffened, then relaxed. Here, as he had already observed, Kaifeng was master. A wise man would accept what could not be prevented; later, perhaps, there would be time to alter the relationship.

"You mentioned—"

"To you, nothing," interrupted Kaifeng. "But words can be sent to where they must go if the route by which they are carried is known. In your war against Terran Control I can give you the means of inevitable mastery."

"War?"

"A word. Let us call it a crusade if that pleases you better. Your race despises the monkey-men, as you call them. You regard it as your destiny to eliminate them from all habitable worlds and engulf the Terran Sphere into your own Complex. If any Terrestrials are permitted to survive it will be as slaves. It is a brave concept, but futile as long as you refuse to recognize that the forces of Terra are more than equal to your own. I offer you the chance of more than redressing the balance."

"At a cost."

"Naturally." Again Kaifeng made the small gesture. The Chambodian couldn't be sure if it was a demand to see the obvious, or an outward display of contempt. "Have you not paused to wonder why your plans have never succeeded? Would you like to know why? The answer is simple—money."

"Are you saying that we are reluctant to spend?"

"On some things, no."

"What then? Do you dare to hint that any Chambodian could be bribed?"

"Every man has his price," said Kaifeng dryly. "A fact Earth has known since earliest history and one the Terrans are not reluctant to use. To them money is cheaper than blood. Later, if we come to an arrangement, I shall show you one of the men you are up against. You will be surprised at what he can tell you."

"If he will talk."

"You doubt my ability?"

For a moment the Chambodian stared into the crimson-flecked emerald eyes, saw the fanatical resolve lurking within their depths, the utter conviction. For the first time he felt himself to be inferior to the other, a sensation he did not like.

"No," he admitted. "If there was doubt as to that I would not be here. But, you understand, I must have proof. That was promised."

"And it will be provided." Kaifeng gestured toward a door. "Everything is ready. Tsing! Accompany our guest to the training area."

It was vast, a tremendous hall cut from the living rock, the vaulted roof set with a battery of Kells, the floor smooth, surrounded by an overhanging balcony. People waited there, an old woman, guards, technicians wearing dull green ornamented with scarlet insignia.

"Laura Previn." Kaifeng lifted a hand, waved for her to come near. "You may have heard of her, a most accomplished woman who has given me the fruits of her genius. Tell our guest what you have developed during your time here."

Old age and a weakened mind, she wanted to answer, but now was not the time to indulge in irony. It would only be wasted on the visitor anyway.

"A means of accelerated clone development from any selected subject coupled with a genetic manipulation which enables the best characteristics of any group of subjects to be incorporated into a unified whole. I take it that you are familiar with biochemical engineering?"

"I am a soldier. Such things are left to our lower caste technicnans."

"Then I shall have to use layman's language and analogies. Any protoplasmic creature begins life as a single cell which incorporates the genetic code and includes the genetic pattern. This is built of chromosomes which carry the genes, that is, the carriers of hereditary traits such as the color of the eyes and hair. With care and skill any set of genes can be assembled within the natural boundaries of the selected species and a new adaption of that species originated. This, when done by natural causes such as exposure of the germ plasm to radiation, gives rise to familiar mutations: children born with an extra limb or lacking a normal organ. Freaks and horrors which, fortunately, are usually unable to survive and even if they do are mostly sterile. Am I boring you?"

"I am aware of mutations." Ges Zalk was curt. "Will you get to the point?"

"If you are sure you can follow me."

The insolence of the woman was intolerable, but she was a member of the despised race and they were noted for their insufferable familiarity.

"You are telling me that you are capable of building a selected creature from relevant genes. That you can improve the species by intent and avoid the failures caused by natural mutation. May I add that among my own people genetic engineering is not unknown."

"Then you are familiar with the Hafeek-Sonda myellium? The endoderm-fallagetes and the Cremsley Coronate? No? Well, never mind. As you say, each to his trade. To put it simply, a means has been found of accelerated cellular division during which the incipient fetus is controlled from the gamete-zygote stage by selected stimuli. This, coupled with forced growth, results in the formation of complete beings within the space of one month from inception."

"A month?"

"Incredible, isn't it?" she said tiredly. "Basically all the essential data was known, all we needed was time in which to pursue certain lines of research, and the master gave us time."

"But a month?"

"From when the installation first begins to operate. The production, naturally, is geared to the extent of the apparatus, but one basic source can provide an indefinite number of clones. Division," she explained. "Two makes four which makes eight and so on. We can arrest normal development by chemical means."

Ges Zalk turned to Kaifeng.

"This is amazing! It takes eighteen years to develop a normal male—and yet this woman claims it can be done within a month. But the tuition and training?"

"The brain can be programmed by selected electronic data," said Kaifeng. "It takes approximately a week for the clone-man to gain full coordination and awareness of himself as a personality. By personality, of course, I am speaking of an awareness of identity. As they are all identical and as each receives the same basic program, all share the same characteristics." He lifted an arm. "But I think that a demonstration at this time will answer most of your questions."

His arm swept down in a signal.

Men filed into the room.

Ges Zalk stared at them, his eyes darting from face to face, momentarily confused. Each was identical to the rest; it was as if he looked into facing mirrors which reflected what was between them over and over again. Fifty men, a hundred, two hundred. They filed into the open area below keeping perfect time, wheeling, adopting new formations, finally coming to rest in mathematically precise lines.

"Note the physical development," said Kaifeng. "Good muscles and strong bones. Equipping them will be simple, one size of everything. The metabolism has been adjusted so that they require the minimum amount of food, a near-complete food-energy cycle which leaves the smallest waste. They are resistant to changes of temperature and need little recreation. A high healing level has been incorporated into their cellular structure and the pain level is extremely high. Allow me to demonstrate." He gave another signal. "Now! Observe!"

A guard moved forward with a loaded whip. As the Chambodian watched he began to lash at the man facing him, the whip leaving ugly welts on the smoothly naked torso. Blood ran over the flesh to stain the loincloth he wore. To any normal man the pain would have been intense, but the product of the vats didn't flinch.

"As you see, they will still remain effective even if badly wounded." Kaifeng turned from the edge of the balcony. "As soldiers they will make superb material, as you have noticed."

"I have?"

"You doubt the evidence of your own eyes?"

"Drilling can be taught," said the Chambodian flatly. "And drugs can raise the pain level to an unnatural height. True, they look alike, but aside from that you have shown me little to impress those I represent."

"Not even the speed of their production?"

"For that, Doctor, I must take your word."

For a moment there was silence, a strained period of waiting during which little sounds became unusually loud, the scrape of a foot, the inhalation of a breath, the quickly suppressed titter from the woman.

Then Kaifeng said coldly, "I assume that you are not calling me a liar. If you are then not even your high position would save you from the penalty of such an insult. But you disappoint me. From others I would have expected such a reaction, but since when has Chambodia turned into a race of haggling merchants?"

"Doctor!"

"To decry the offered product is the habit of common traders. Obviously I made a mistake in approaching your council. Still, there are others who will be more interested."

"Please, wait!" Ges Zalk lifted a hand in appeal. If he should fail this mission all hope of future advancement would be lost. "Doctor, you misunderstood me. I was simply being cautious. Surely I cannot be blamed for that?"

"For caution? No. Are there any special tests you would like to have made? Field operations are obviously out of the question, but anything else?"

Laura Previn said, "How about courage?"

With relief Ges Zalk turned toward her, conscious that he had made a mistake, had stepped too close to the edge of danger in more ways than one. But a lifetime of command had made it difficult for him to accept a member of any other race as more than an inferior. With this woman, at least, he would not have to watch his words.

"Courage? Of course. How could it be demonstrated?"

"Set them against each other. Have them kill and die. Let them see blood and feel pain."

"But the whip?"

"A slave will stand unmoving beneath a whip. Do you want an army of slaves?"

It was a good point. Soldiers should be aggressive, not humble, and had the man been all that was claimed he surely would have defended himself against the guard.

He said, "Doctor, with your permission, I would like them to do as the woman says."

"As you wish." Kaifeng gestured toward the guards below. "They will fight and they will die. Let them begin."

They moved like the stroked pages of a book, each moving at exactly the same pace, alternate ranks turning to face the one behind, space growing between individuals. For a moment they stared at each other and then, like the meshed components of a machine, the clone-men lifted their fists, struck, reeled beneath blows, struck again in a rising fury of action and then, abruptly, broke ranks and ran in frenzied panic.

Ges Zalk stared his disbelief as they raced for the exits, thrusting aside guards, some falling to rise screaming with fear.

"Cowards," he said blankly. "They are all cowards. Are these your vaunted troops, Doctor?"

"You!" Kaifeng stared at Laura Previn. "You are responsible for this!"

Her laugh rose high, triumphant above the noise.

"My revenge, *Master!*" The title was a sneer. "And it was so easily done. An adjustment of the genes, an induced factor which triggers a panic-reaction when the adrenalin level reaches a certain point. They, all of them, are useless. And you didn't know. You didn't know!"

"Guards!"

"You intend to kill me," she said backing toward the edge of the balcony. "But I won't die alone. You, all of you, will come with me. Lars Horsen is detonating the power plant!"

CHAPTER THIRTEEN

The first shock came as Kennedy reached the foot of the shaft leading upward, a twitch of the floor followed by a prolonged rumbling, the air darkened with a shower of drifting motes of dust. Through it ran near-naked men, the panic-stricken clones, followed by guards armed with Diones. One halted close to where Kennedy stood, not seeing the girl behind him, catching only a glimpse of a familiar uniform.

The air seemed to burn as the guard fired, drifting dust specks flaring into incandescence. A livid shaft of eye-bright radiance reached from the flared muzzle to touch a running clone-man on the back, to sear through him so that, for a moment, he hung suspended on a rod of flame.

The roar of the discharge filled the passage as Kennedy stepped forward, the bar he held a glinting whirl cutting through the air to smash the back of the guard's head to a pulp. As he fell Kennedy caught the Dione and threw it toward Vivien.

"Cover me."

"Right, Cap."

A small chamber opened from the passage, obviously a guard room, now empty. Kennedy picked up the dead man and carried him inside, stripping off his uniform. He took the Dione from the girl's hand and said, "Change. Put on that uniform. You can't wear a suit over that robe and we need the camouflage."

"What's happening, Cap?"

"Laura Previn managed to persuade her friends to blow up the installation. They must have detonated the chemical store or the reserve power supply. We've got to get out before the atomics let loose." He sprang aside as a mass of stone fell from the roof, adding to the dust in the air, dimming the glow of the Kells with a roiling fog. "Ready yet?"

"Yes." She came toward him, fumbling with the belt. "How do you work this thing?"

"There's a button at the top, aim it and press, but don't bother with it, use this." He handed her the Dione. "Let's get moving."

The passage was filled with noise, echoes rolling flatly from the stone, muted by the thick clouds of dust. A second tremor came, more violent than the first, Kells falling to break and lie in dull patches, their loss accentuating the gloom.

Shadows came through it, running guards who passed without comment, except for one who came to a halt and stared at the couple.

"Don't stand there! Emergency procedure! Hurry!" His eyes widened as the dust thinned a little and he saw the glint of Vivien's hair. "Who are you? What—"

He tried to lift his Dione too late. Kennedy was on him before it could level, one hand gripping the finned barrel and pushing it safely aside, the other lifting to sweep down in a killing blow.

"Cap!"

"Come on. Follow close and don't hesitate to fire."

Gun in one hand, the bar in the other, Kennedy led the way up the shaft. It curved, narrowing, the end sealed by a grille of thick bars. The door was firmly locked. Beyond it he could see a chamber flanked with instruments, the panels a mass of winking lights.

It was a dead end, and the worst kind of trap. They would be caught in opposing fire if guards came up from below and there were men in the room.

Kennedy turned and saw Vivien's anxious face. Dust had streaked her hair and smudged her eyes, but the gun in her hand was firm and he knew she could use it.

"Cap?"

"We took the wrong turning. It's an observation post of some kind. We'll have to try again."

The noise below had increased. He stepped back as a bunch of clone-men raced past, catching the smell of their fear. A third shock, more savage than the others, ripped stone from the roof and crushed the clones in crimson heaps. A wall collapsed to reveal a wide chamber, the shapes of guards.

They carried a casket with Valdemar at their side, his thin voice querulous.

"Be careful! You mustn't hurt her! She needs to be handled with care!"

One of the guards turned and smashed the back of his hand against Valdemar's face. The old man fell, blood on his mouth and chin, his eyes wild.

"Help me!" he called as Kennedy ran toward him. "Help me! She—" He broke off, frowning, shaking his head. "I know you. I've seen you before."

"Where are they taking the girl?"

"Away. They're taking her away."

"Where?" Kennedy stooped, gripped a thin shoulder, shook it with mounting urgency. "To the air lock? Where?"

"I don't know. Kaifeng—I don't know."

He screamed as a blast tore through the chamber. Air whined, dust swirled, fragments of razor-sharp stones tore at the flesh, the eyes. The roar of the explosion was magnified by the walls of the cavern, shock waves sending out responsive echoes so the very air shook and quivered. It felt as if they were standing in the center of a gigantic bell.

Kennedy rolled, feeling blood on his mouth, his chin, more spilling from his nose. Vivien lay huddled to one side, her arms over her head, crimson from her ears staining her hair. She turned as he reached for her, opening her eyes, her hands closing around his neck as if for comfort.

"Cap, what happened? Your face!"

"Concussion." He dabbed at the blood, wiping it off

on a sleeve, and felt the sting of tiny cuts. The girl had been more fortunate; aside from the blood at her ears she was unmarked.

Valdemar was dead.

He lay like a discarded bundle of rags. One arm was lifted, his face distorted from inner pressure, the eyes bulging, the tongue thrust between swollen lips. Dust lay thick on his face, filling the seams until he seemed to be wearing a grotesque mask.

"Cap?"

"We've got to get out. The next thing to go might be the atomics." Kennedy stood, eyes searching the area, memory trying to fit the broken walls, the littered chamber into a remembered pattern. The guards had vanished with their burden through an arched opening in the far end of the room. Beyond it must lie an entry port, suits and a means of escape. "Stay close, Vivien. If I start shooting join in and don't hesitate."

That was a thing easier said than done by those unaccustomed to violence, but Kennedy knew the girl was a trained agent and would not hesitate if the need arose.

"Cap, do you think we've got a chance?"

"We're alive," he said curtly, and it was answer enough. While there was life there was always hope. He wiped again at his face. "Come on."

Beyond the arch was a wide passage. This soon branched, one opening almost solidly blocked by fallen stone, the other thick with dust in which faint marks showed. He took the latter, ran up a ramp and saw a door closing before him. It thudded shut before he could reach it and he turned, eyes narrowed as he looked up and around. Broken stone showed where steps had risen from the floor to an opening about thirty feet above the floor—the only way out other than the entrance they had used.

He threw the bar toward the girl.

"Cut it in half with your Dione. Quickly!"

As she obeyed he fired at the wall, echoes rolling as he pressed the trigger, red spots glowing in the sheer wall of stone, molten rock dripping from the point of impact to cool in wax-like extrusions. A series of holes reached up toward the opening above.

The gun in his belt, a half-length of bar in each hand, he snapped, "Get on my back and hang on. Don't choke me and keep your gun handy. If you see anything in that opening fire immediately."

The precaution was useless, for once started they would be helpless targets. With Vivien on his back Kennedy stepped to the wall, thrust a bar into one of the holes, the other higher up. Hanging on it he removed the first bar and rammed it home into a hole burned above the second. Slowly, sweat turning the dust on his face into a gritty mud, back and shoulder muscles taut against the fabric of his tunic, he inched his way upward.

As they reached the opening Vivien fired.

Kennedy tensed, hearing the scream echoing the roar of discharge, feeling something topple from above, to hit his left hand, to tear it from the bar, the bar from the hole, to brush against them with muscle-tearing force.

Hanging suspended, one hand locked around the remaining bar, the weight of the girl dragging at his shoulders, he waited until their pendulum-like motion had stilled.

"Up, Vivien, but be careful!"

Like a cat she climbed up his body, resting one foot on his head as she lunged into the opening. Slowly he drew himself upward, hooked his chin over the end of the bar, then his left elbow, balancing on his extended left arm as his right lifted to grip the rim of the opening. A surge and he was up and standing beside the girl. She was unarmed—the falling body had knocked the Dione from her hand. Kennedy felt at his belt; his own gun had been lost during the final upward scramble.

"We'll have to depend on bluff. Tie back your hair, Vivien, and plaster it with dust. Your face too." She was already dirty, but more would mask the softly feminine outlines. The too large uniform already masked her figure. "That's it." Kennedy looked at the floor of the passage. Little swirls moved the dust, lifted it in tiny plumes.

She said, "I can feel a breeze, Cap. The air's moving."

It wasn't moving, it was escaping, gushing into the void through a fractured seal. The wind increased as they ran down the passage, rock dust rising to choke their lungs and sting their eyes. It strengthened as they burst into a chamber thick with guards. A dead man lay on the floor, a Chambodian, a hole charred between the eyes.

"Here!" A guard was handing out emergency suits, thin envelopes of transparent plastic fitted with limited tanks. "Get into these and go down to sector nine. The passage is blocked from here. Move!"

Suited, Kennedy looked around. The inner door of an air lock stood to his right, a bunch of armed guards to his left. One of them stepped forward, gesturing.

"Hurry, you two. The master will punish any who delay."

Kennedy said, "A minute, this seal . . ." He tugged at the helmet and then, dropping his hand, thrust home the button on the box-buckle at his belt.

The suit provided no barrier to the electronic whip. Aimed at the guards, it sent them falling, rolling in muscular agony. Before they could recover he was at the port, jerking open the door, slamming it as Vivien followed him into the lock.

Together they ran over a night time surface, jagged with uplifted spears of ebony stone. The gulleys between were filled with a crystalline substance that crushed beneath their boots.

"Cap!" Vivien caught Kennedy's arm, sound transmitted by the direct contact. "Cap, they're coming!"

A dozen suited figures leaped over the terrain, guns lifted. Shafts of flame seared the rocks to either side, passed overhead as Kennedy and Vivien ducked.

Kennedy ran along the gulley, drew back as a guard fired, lunged forward as he moved out of sight, always trying to keep jagged pinacles between the guards and themselves.

Kennedy knew he was playing a desperate game of hide and seek with death the penalty should he lose. And nowhere could he see the *Mordain*.

CHAPTER FOURTEEN

"Jarl!" Chemile's voice echoed his anxiety. "I'm not getting Cap's signal. Have you anything on the monitors?"

"Not yet, Veem." Luden worriedly examined his instruments. Before them the dull shape of the planetoid occluded distant stars. It was a bleak, savage place shaped like an egg, the long axis stretching a hundred miles, the surface scarred, enigmatic. Like a wary animal the *Mordain* had drifted toward it, the ports masked, the engines silent, nothing but the scanners alive. "The gulleys seem to be filled with some form of electromagnetic baffle, probably a natural crystalline deposit with a broad-spectrum refractive index. If Cap is within the base his signal could be blocked or so blurred that it merges with the general pattern."

"If?" Saratov's rumble carried the general concern. "This has to be Kaifeng's base, Jarl. Where else would they have taken Cap?"

"Probably nowhere, Penza, but the possibility remains that the ship we saw may have taken him to another world." Luden adjusted a control. "The likelihood is remote, I admit, but other things could have happened."

. . . Such as Kennedy taken, killed, dissected. The transmitter found and destroyed. A prison fitted with opaque screens. A dozen things.

"We should move in closer," said the giant. "Even if the signal is being diffused we might still be able to pick it up."

"That planetoid has a surface area of over a million

square miles, Penza," said Luden thinly. "The closer we get the less of it we can scan, and also the greater the risk we run of being discovered. In fact I can't understand why we haven't already been detected. The observers may be accustomed to drifting masses of debris, but once we engage power and alter course it will be obvious what we are."

"Cap may be keeping them busy," said Saratov grimly. "But he'll need our help. Why can't we go in, Jarl, and give them more to think about?"

The temptation to go in was great, to create a distraction, to destroy, but action without purpose was both stupid and dangerous. Luden made another adjustment to his instruments, narrowing their focus, his eyes fastened on the monitor. Chemile's voice blasted from the speaker.

"Jarl! The signal!"

"I can see it, Veem."

"Then we go in!" Saratov's voice was a roar. "If that's Cap he needs us. Move, Veem!"

"Wait!" Luden was less impulsive. "Cap could still be within the planetoid. There could be a weak point in the natural baffle." He drew in his breath as the glowing spot on the grid began to move, to blink in a rapid series of on-off pulses—the compact code which resolved all doubts.

"Move, Veem! Penza, stand by the guns! Cap's signaling and he's in trouble!"

The *Mordain* became alive, engines pulsing with unleashed power. The jagged ovoid of the planetoid expanded as Chemile sent the ship hurtling toward it, aiming at the point where the signal flared and died, flared again. Details grew on the screens, clear in magnification, twin shapes crouching in a gulley, others coming close, firing as they came.

"Penza!"

"Got it, Jarl!"

In the turret Saratov aligned the sights and, as Chemile brought the *Mordain* down close and level with the ground, he tripped the release of the Dione. A handgun could burn a hole through a man, holding enough power to incinerate a horse; the heavy-duty model carried in the turret could puddle a mansion with a single shot. Like the blast of a furnace it swept the rocks clean, turning men into motes of ash and transient radiance, searing away the crystalline deposits and causing jagged peaks to slump in rounded mounds.

"Cap!" Vivien's helmet was touching his own, her voice betraying her fear. The blast had come too close for comfort—a fraction of misalignment and they would have joined the guards.

"It's all right, Vivien. It's the *Mordain*."

"But to fire so close!"

"They had no choice." Kennedy watched as the vessel turned, firing again, the last of their pursuers falling beneath the discharge. As it came toward them, settling, the port already open, he rose and took her hand. "Come on, Vivien. Run!"

Luden met them as they entered the ship, his eyes widening as Kennedy stripped off the suit.

"Cap! Your face! Are you hurt?"

"Scratches, dirt and dried blood. Veem! Take evasive action."

"Already done, Cap," said Chemile cheerfully as he sent the *Mordain* upward, veering to dodge any missile which might have been aimed at them. "How's the girl?"

"Fine. Jarl, put her in a cabin. Penza, get to the engines; I'll relieve Veem at the controls as he takes over the guns. Full power to the screens. Action stations!"

The *Mordain* prepared for combat like a well-oiled machine, reports coming with sharp precision.

"Defensive screens at optimum, Cap."

"Life-support and damage-control functioning."

"Guns ready." Chemile was eager for action. "This time we'll get Kaifeng and get him for good."

"I hope so, Veem." Kennedy checked the controls. The initial burst of speed had carried them well away from the planetoid; now he turned and headed back toward it. "Jarl, did you spot any vessels leaving the area?"

"No, Cap."

"Good, then Kaifeng must still be inside the base. We'll make a quick pass. Somewhere close to where you picked us up must be a large air lock—Kaifeng needed it to pass his ship inside. It will be coming out, and when it does I want to get it."

"An assumption, Cap?"

"A certainty, Jarl. The atomic units powering the base are due to blow at any moment. At least they will if Laura Previn's friends finish what they started. Kaifeng can't take the risk that they'll fail. He will leave the base. Ready, Veem?"

"Ready."

"Fire three torps at where you picked us up. Now!"

Kennedy hit a button, the stars flickering as he reached plus-C velocity, flickering again as the automatic cutoffs went into operation. The bulk of the planetoid was before them immediately, torpedoes streaking toward the surface to explode in gouts of atomic destruction.

Blue fire sparked at points beyond the holocaust and the *Mordain* jerked as if kicked by an invisible boot.

The screens flared, then again showed the vista of space as new scanners cut in to replace those ruined. Again came the blue fire, missing as Kennedy sent the ship up and away. Behind them space writhed with the release of destructive energies.

"Penza?"

"The screens took a beating, Cap, but they are holding at eighty percent efficiency."

"Jarl?"

"Life-support system intact. Minor damage to the rear lower left quadrant. Compartment fourteen holed but sealed."

"They've got teeth," said Chemile grimly. "The entire base is built like a fortress, but if we hit the air lock it will be useless now."

Kennedy absorbed the reports with only part of his mind, the rest concentrating on the planetoid. It was too big for him to destroy totally and he could only guess at the extent of the defensive installations. If a MALACA had been close the entire bulk of the tiny world could have been turned into incandescent vapor. But he had only the *Mordain,* and its destructive power had to be conserved for use against the ship which could still appear.

This time Kaifeng must not escape.

Luden said, "Cap, Kaifeng's vessel is incredibly fast. When we tried to follow it before we couldn't keep up. There is a mystery about its screens which I hope to later resolve, but the point is that you will have little time in which to make an attack."

"Suggestions, Jarl?"

"If the base is about to explode as you say, it might be better to confine the vessel somehow."

"Agreed, which is why the attempt was made to seal the lock."

But the lock area could only occupy a minute fraction of the surface of the planetoid. Kennedy leaned forward and increased the magnification of the screens. To one side of where the three torps had struck a thin haze grew, air gusting into space, expanding, softening naturally bleak outlines.

That fracture could open into the buried air lock itself, or it could be the forerunner of the explosion which should have already occurred. There were only seconds to make a decision.

"Veem, ready all torps, aim directly ahead when I give the word."

"Right, Cap."

It was a chance, but one which had to be taken, a calculated gamble. If it succeeded, Kaifeng's vessel would be smashed between the hammer of the overdue explosion and the anvil of the *Mordain*'s torpedoes. Those opposed forces would defeat the toughest screens ever devised.

Kennedy rested his hands on the controls, becoming a living extension of the vessel, trained reflexes unhampered by the slowing need for conscious thought. The blurred point came closer as he waited, calculating time and distance, eyes narrowed for signs of a familiar, glinting shape. Something seemed to move directly ahead, a spurt of blue, a shimmer, something.

"Now, Veem!"

As the torps flashed from their launchers Kennedy heard Luden's shout.

"Cap! The planetoid!"

A red glow marred the dull surface, a savage light which expanded into a searing, spreading blue-white glare. Masses of broken rubble rose above the sphere, stone pulverized by the force of the internal explosion—a released hell aggravated by the torpedoes, which added their atomic chaos to the fury already released in the base.

The *Mordain* spun, turning end over end, all control lost in the impact of the shock wave. The hull rang like a bell as a hail of shattered particles slammed against the metal. Scanners burned out. Blind, the screens ruined, Kennedy fought to regain mastery of the vessel.

"Jarl?"

"Major circuits burned out, Cap. Emergency function only. Hull intact."

"Penza?"

"Screens down. Some engine damage, but I can adjust the coils to get us moving at about seventy percent of optimum efficiency. How's Veem?"

"Lucky," said Chemile. "I was using full filters. Our torps accentuated the inner explosion and triggered disruption of the released vapor. Right, Jarl?"

"You are probably correct, Veem," said Luden dryly. "Certainly nothing in that area of the planetoid could possibly have survived."

Laura Previn and the others, the woman too—the fantastically lovely girl he had seen in the casket, the product of stolen skills and warped genius—were gone. She, all of them, were turned into blazing atoms.

But the living still remained.

Vivien was very pale, yet she tried to be casual. "What happened, Cap, did Kaifeng try to bite back?"

"His base did." Kennedy looked at the monitoring screens in the cabin, new scanners showing the distant bulk of the planetoid, the ugly red glow at one end. "A little closer and we would have been volatilized with the installation."

"I'm glad that we weren't, Cap. So very glad."

She stepped toward him, smiling. She had washed and changed into some of his spare clothing, the arms and legs rolled up, a sash binding her waist. She was a woman who was going to enjoy the journey back to Weingold, who knew that once they landed each would go their own way. She accepted it—it would be a rare woman who could hold Kennedy for long.